CH00806756

About the Author

Pam Lecky hails from Dublin, Ireland, and has been an avid reader of historical fiction from an early age. Then one day she decided that reading wasn't enough and she started to write. Her first published novel, *The Bowes Inheritance*, was the result and she hasn't stopped writing since.

Praise for *The Bowes Inheritance*

"*The Bowes Inheritance* is a stunning, captivating and all-round brilliant first novel." Historical Novel Society Review

Readers' Reviews

Being a Georgette Heyer fan, I didn't think I would ever find a writer who would captivate me to the same extent. However, *The Bowes Inheritance* has renewed my love for historical fiction

*****

Beautifully written with a page turning plot

*****

A thrilling and entertaining story

*****

An enjoyable, well researched and well written novel

PAST IMPERFECT

A COLLECTION OF SHORT STORIES

હ

PAM LECKY

ISBN-13: 978-1983633485
ISBN-10: 1983633488

Copyright © Pam Lecky 2018

All rights reserved.
No part of this publication may be reproduced, stored in a
retrieval system or transmitted, in any form or by any means,
without the prior written permission of the author, nor be
otherwise circulated in any form of binding or cover other
than that in which it is published and without a similar
condition being imposed on the purchaser.

Past Imperfect is a work of fiction. Names, characters, places
and incidents are the products of the author's imagination or
are used fictitiously. Any resemblance to actual events, locales
or persons, living or dead, is entirely coincidental.

www.pamlecky.com

Cover Image: ©iStock.com/heckmannoleg

In memory of my parents,
Betty & Gerry Lecky,
who instilled in me a love
of reading and history.

Contents

In Three-Quarter Time   1

The Lighthouse Keeper   23

The Promise   45

The Gift   63

Mayday   69

Christmas at Malton Manor   77

In Three-Quarter Time

Dublin, September 1914

Sunday afternoon tea was a ritual for the Cusack family. In the parlour, the table was covered in the best lace tablecloth and the Royal Albert tea service came out of the sideboard. The younger siblings still lived at home, but Lily and Margaret had their own flat on Baggot Street. Every Sunday they would hop on a tram and journey across the Liffey as far as Nelson's Pillar. Home, which was situated above their father's tobacconist shop in North Earl Street, was only a short walk away.

"I can't imagine where Will has got to," Mother said, after greeting the girls. "The tea is just made."

Margaret picked up the teapot. "Up to mischief, no doubt!" she exclaimed, winking at Lily behind Mother's back. Lily bent down and kissed her mother's soft cheek and breathed in the comforting scent of lilac. She linked her arm and they followed Margaret into the parlour. Father and their younger sister, Josie, were already seated at the table.

Father looked up expectantly. "Ah," he said with a frown. "I thought it was William. Come and kiss your father, girls."

They both did so and took their usual places. Lily immediately noticed how pale Josie looked.

"It is most unlike Will. I wonder where he could have got to?" Mother said as she sat down.

"No doubt he will turn up shortly, but I think we will go ahead," Father said, looking none too pleased. After saying grace he turned to Josie. "We seem to be missing another young man. Why do we not have the pleasure of Anthony's company today? This must be the first Sunday in over a year that he has not joined us."

"It's the last weekend before he leaves for America and he wanted to spend it with his mother and sister," Josie said. Lily's heart sank. She had dreaded coming home today, for she knew that Anthony's departure was sure to be a topic of conversation. All week she had tried not to think about him leaving and the possibility that she might never see him again.

"It's what I'd expect of him, but his poor mother must be distraught at the prospect of him leaving the country. So he is determined to carry through with this plan of his?"

"Yes, he leaves next weekend," Josie said. She bent her head and her delicate fingers crumbled her pastry into tiny pieces. Lily did feel sorry for her. Anthony had only broken the news to her the week before.

"But he will come back, my dear. You must not fret about it," Mother said gently, though she caught Lily's eye and shook her head slightly. Everyone assumed the big romance was over.

"I don't understand it," Father said, oblivious to the pleading looks that Mother began sending across the table. "He has a great job and a lovely young lady …" This was directed at Josie, who looked up and gave him a weak smile. "And now with war declared it's hardly the time to go gallivanting around the world."

"I imagine he has been planning to leave for some time and long before all this trouble in Europe," Lily said. "Everyone says America is the land of opportunity. It must be a very exciting place."

Father narrowed his eyes. "You're not thinking of emigrating too?"

"No, of course not," Lily lied. She had thought of little else since learning of Anthony's plans to emigrate.

"It's a heathen place and not somewhere I'd want any daughter of mine," he said with a furrowing of his brows.

"And," he bobbed his head, "they have that modern music – what's it called?"

"Ragtime," Lily said.

"Yes – that's it. Godless music! Now what is wrong with a waltz, I ask you? You can't get more romantic than that, girls - a lovely melody in three-quarter time. Isn't that right, Mother? That giddy stuff will never take on."

Lily felt a kick land on her shin. Margaret's face was the picture of innocence, but she wasn't fooled. Father had some very odd notions. It was best not to tell him they frequented a dance club every Saturday night where ragtime was the music of choice.

"There was a waltz playing the night I met Tony," Josie said with a sigh. Lily could feel Margaret's eyes on her, but refused to engage. Josie's sentimentality was tiresome, but she was young and Lily half envied her naiveté. She also envied her Anthony and for the past six months had been struggling with her own feelings. It was shameful and there was no one she could tell. There was no one who would understand.

"You see! I'm right," Father continued on a triumphant note. "And speaking of Anthony, he should know we need all the men at home, ready to fight. Mr Murphy told me conscription is very likely."

"But Father," Lily said, "I've seen the crowds outside the recruiting office on Brunswick Street. There doesn't appear to be any shortage of volunteers to take the King's shilling."

"Aye, well most of those boyos have been out of work since the Lockout, last year. They have been blacklisted and have no choice but to sign up," her father said. "I only hope they prove loyal to the crown but I wouldn't trust those socialists an inch."

"Their families must be starving," Lily said, feeling the need to defend them. His sympathies had been with the employers throughout the troubles. She could not believe he was oblivious to the poverty in the tenements which were only a street away. The gulf between the rich and poor was impossible to ignore. The reasons were manifold and events the previous summer had only made things worse. The city was crawling with wretched souls trying to scrape a living. Even the children had a look of desperation. She had often seen them rooting in bins for food or looking for clinkers of coal in the ash thrown out by the wealthy. She could not bear to look them in the eye, even as she gave them what she could.

"Those men chose to walk away from their jobs and over a few pennies per hour," Father continued. "There were plenty of hard-working men to take their place. That Jim Larkin has a lot to answer for, if you ask me!"

"Now, my dears, this is hardly the time or the place," Mother intervened with a sharp glance directed at her. Lily shrugged. It was an old argument and one she could not win.

Father cleared his throat. "I do hope the threat of conscription isn't the reason Anthony's leaving?"

Josie's face went bright red. "Absolutely not! Father, you know he is in the Citizen Army. You saw the injuries he sustained last year. He's no coward."

"Rest easy, child," Father said gently. "No need to fire up like that. Sure I know him well enough and what he has done, though I cannot say I approve of his politics."

The sound of the front door opening was swiftly followed by the entrance of Will into the parlour. Lily looked up as the room fell into stunned silence for he was wearing the uniform of a Dublin Fusilier.

Mother went deadly pale. "Will, what have you done?" she cried, half rising up, her knuckles white where they clutched the edge of the table.

"Signed up, of course, Mother." He laughed and gave a twirl. "Well, ladies, what do you think?"

No one answered.

Will pursed his lips. "Well, I thought I'd get a better reception than this."

Father stood up and held out his hand. "We're surprised, that's all. Isn't that so, girls? I'm proud of you, my boy," he said, his voice shaking and his eyes suspiciously bright.

Lily watched an array of emotions flit across her mother's face, too, but she saw her fingers curl around her napkin in distress. She reached over and touched her hand in support.

Father beamed. "I believe this is cause for a celebration. Margaret, fetch the sherry!"

The following Friday evening after work, Lily and Margaret were sipping their cocoa before the fire in their own flat.

"What is so amusing?" Margaret asked.

"Well, not so much amusing as tragic. You know I called in to see Mother last night?" she answered. "You should have heard the rumpus Josie was making."

"Hysterics again?"

"Yes indeed. 'Why is he deserting me? He'll meet someone else.' And of course, Mother was pandering to her."

"Making it worse!"

She nodded. "If Father had been there she would not have gone on so. At least he seems to wield some control over her. She has been over-indulged and all because she nearly died as a child. If it were you or me, we would be told to grow up. There is poor Mother worried sick about Will and the scrape he no doubt will get himself into. But does Josie give her a moment's thought? No! I eventually got her to calm down but, my God, I wanted to box her ears."

"I don't blame you. I have often felt the same," Margaret said with a wicked grin.

Lily blew out her cheeks and settled into a more comfortable position, pulling her shawl more closely around her shoulders.

"Do you think Anthony will come back?" she asked as nonchalantly as she could. Margaret was the level-headed one, but also as sharp as an eagle. If she ever suspected what her feelings were, there would be holy war.

"Who knows, Lil – Josie's predictions may come true. He will be far from home with only her letters and a photograph

5

to remind him of her and three years is a long time to wait. If some pretty young thing decides to bring him comfort, there is little Josie can do about it."

"I suppose you may have the right of it," Lily said. She stared into the flames as a black despair descended, for she shared Josie's fears.

Dublin was wilting in an Indian summer. To the west, a bank of steel grey cloud hung low on the horizon and the air was heavy with the promise of a storm. Lily looked up at the raucous gulls wheeling above the Liffey and wrinkled her nose at the strong and disagreeable smell wafting up from the water. The quays were never a pleasant place to linger on a hot day but they were waiting at the tram stop for Anthony. They had arranged to accompany him to Kingsbridge Station where he would board the train for Queenstown and from there the boat to America.

It was a busy Saturday afternoon and the cobbles echoed to the sound of horse hooves and the rattle and hiss of trams. Josie paced up and down, her cheeks pinched and pale, her eyes scanning the sluggish stream of pedestrians going about their business.

"Could we have missed him?" Josie asked. She checked her watch again. "It's already a quarter to. Perhaps we should go to Kingsbridge and check if he is there already?"

"Don't fret. I imagine he has been delayed saying goodbye to his family," she said, trying to hide her impatience.

Josie gave her an apologetic smile. "Of course, that would be it – his mother is too unwell to travel to the station to see him off." She resumed her pacing. Lily wished Josie didn't always wear her heart on her sleeve. A little dignity would not go amiss.

Lily changed position and wished she had worn more comfortable shoes. As she turned, she caught a glimpse of herself in the window of McBirney's Department Store. Her reflection did nothing to improve her mood. Her hair clung in damp curls to the side of her face and the cream linen suit, which had seemed an excellent choice that morning, was looking limp and sadly wrinkled. She was no beauty, like Josie or Margaret, but she prided herself on always looking her best. She straightened her hat, tucked a stray red curl behind her ear and turned back towards Josie.

Moments later, a familiar voice hailed them from the other side of the quay. "Hello, hello," Anthony called from across the street.

Josie gave a little squeak of joy and Lily's heart leapt. It was difficult not to admire him – so tall and distinguished. His dark hair and skin gave him a foreign look; unusual in Dubliners who were renowned for their pastiness. She watched as he ducked with ease between the trams, carriages and carts. When he reached them he dropped his suitcase to the pavement and shook hands with both of them, his touch strong and sure. Then he removed his black fedora, wiped his brow with a snow-white handkerchief, and grinned. Lily thought he had the look of an eager puppy bent on mischief.

"Thanks for waiting. I hoped you would," he said to Josie. "It was a regular circus at home: my brother Joe and his wife turned up. Such a send-off!"

"I'm sure they will miss you very much, Tony," Josie said, her voice sounding strained.

"Mother will, for sure," he said, not looking the least worried. "But Joe has promised to keep an eye on her."

"I'll look in on her, too, if you'd like?" Josie asked.

Anthony waved his hand. "Only if it suits; she wouldn't expect it." He looked skyward and, much to Lily's irritation, didn't notice how Josie's face fell. "Good lord, that looks rather nasty," he said with a frown. "I hope we reach Kingsbridge before it breaks."

A crackle of electricity announced the arrival of their tram. "Just in time," Lily murmured and Anthony nodded.

"Best stay downstairs," he said, as he ushered them on.

Josie beckoned to Anthony to sit beside her and Lily

slipped into the seat behind. She was annoyed and feeling ridiculous. She was only accompanying them at Father's insistence. The role of duenna did not sit well for many reasons. At twenty-three she enjoyed a measure of freedom. She worked as a typist in a solicitor's office and earned enough to share the flat with Margaret. It seemed ridiculous that Josie could not accompany Anthony alone as far as the station but Father wouldn't hear of it. There had been a scene, the result of which was Lily had to give up her precious Saturday afternoon off. The only advantage was that she would get to see Anthony one more time.

Soon the lovers' heads were together, shoulders touching and they spoke in urgent tones. Surreptitiously, she watched their reflection in the window, oblivious to the passing shops and pedestrians. Josie with her blonde hair and delicate complexion contrasted sharply with Anthony's looks. There was no denying they were a striking couple. He was in high spirits, his beautiful hands moving animatedly as he spoke of his plans to a rapt Josie. Lily looked down and counted to ten, breathing slowly. This was torture.

Josie had told the family he intended to work hard for two or three years and make enough money for them to get married on his return. However, there had been no suggestion of an engagement and just as well, for Father would not have countenanced it under the circumstances. Lily didn't know how she would cope if Anthony became her brother-in-law. It would be utterly unbearable.

He had been walking out with Josie for a year and the family had taken to him quickly. Even Father, who tended to treat all gentleman callers with suspicion, declared him to be a fine young man. Anthony's wit and charm soon endeared him to Mother, too, and he became a regular visitor. With a love of music and a fine voice, he often entertained the family around the piano. It was on one such occasion Lily had realised her true feelings. But he belonged to Josie. Since then she had tried to avoid him, but without much success. He seemed to haunt her parents' house. She dreaded the odd hollow feeling that overcame her when he was near. Luckily, with such a boisterous family, her self-conscious reticence whenever he was present was not remarked on.

Soon they were passing the gates of Guinness's and the façade of Kingsbridge Station came into view, dominating the skyline. The forecourt was busy with a tight press of cabs and trams near the entrance. Large groups of soldiers stood about. Lily guessed they had arrived by train from the Curragh Camp. A large recruitment poster was pasted to one of the pillars at the entrance. Lord Kitchener was pointing his finger, urging men to rise to their country's call.

"Didn't his mother ever tell him it is rude to point," Anthony quipped. Josie giggled.

Lily looked around nervously. It was foolish to make such a comment in public, particularly with army personnel in close proximity. For weeks now there had been nothing but the talk of war and she was weary of it. The turmoil in Europe over the summer had left her bewildered and worried for the future and now Will was soon to depart to England for training. The thought of him facing danger in the field of battle kept her awake at night. That and Anthony leaving.

As they made their way into the entrance hall, they had to stand back as another company of soldiers marched past, laden down with their kit bags.

"There they go – lambs to the slaughter!" Anthony said, with a nod of his handsome dark head towards the last of them.

"Oh hush, Tony, you shouldn't say that," Josie replied, wide-eyed. Lily smarted at his thoughtlessness. He knew Will had signed up.

"It isn't a game, Josie. War is an ugly business, not a romantic crusade," he said. "Thousands will die."

"But everyone says it will be over in a few months," exclaimed Josie, clutching his arm.

Anthony shook his head. "I very much doubt it."

Lily thought he was probably right, but his comments were ill-judged and untimely. The men who had passed had looked so young and full of enthusiasm and Will would soon be joining them.

"So you are prepared to fight for your fellow workers but don't believe in fighting for your country, Mr Lanigan?" Lily asked.

Anthony turned with a bleak smile. "Those workers I helped defend were my fellow Irishmen, Miss Cusack. I'll not fight for the British – 'tis their war, not ours."

She shrugged, trying to control the urge to argue it out with him. It was common knowledge he was a Nationalist but she had never heard him speak openly of his beliefs. Politics was a topic avoided in the Cusack house on a Sunday afternoon. She had wondered why he was leaving, but was certain it was ambition, not cowardice that was driving him. It was somewhat ironic that he had left his job in an army outfitter on Dame Street. They must be snowed under with work with war declared and he just ups and leaves.

"I say, which is the Cork train?" Anthony asked a passing porter.

"Platform four, sir," the man said, pointing to the furthest platform.

Anthony took Josie's gloved hand in his. "This is it, Josie," he said, suddenly solemn.

Lily stood apart as the couple said their goodbyes. Averting her eyes, she watched the soldiers lining up outside the station. There would be no sweethearts to wave them off at Kingstown as they boarded the troopships for England – that seemed so unfair.

She heard footsteps behind her and looked round. He had come up to her and was holding out his hand. "Take good care of her, Miss Cusack," he said, his blue eyes glowing. "Goodbye to you."

She could tell he was impatient to be off on his adventure. Somehow she managed to shake his hand and respond in an even voice. "Safe trip, Mr Lanigan," she said, instead of 'Take me with you' which had suddenly popped into her head.

Josie was rummaging in her bag. Lily pulled her handkerchief from her pocket and handed it to her. "Use mine," she said. Josie gave her a watery smile of thanks.

"Ladies, till we meet again!" he said with a flourish, before picking up his suitcase. "I'll write as soon as I get to New York, Josie."

There was an uncomfortable tightness in Lily's throat and she clenched her hands to stop herself from weeping. Please God, don't let me make a fool of myself, she thought.

She heard Josie sniffle beside her as they watched him walk towards the barrier. She put her arm around her shoulders. "Be brave, Josie," she said. "You'll make it awfully hard for him if he sees you are upset."

"I can't help it," Josie sobbed.

"Be thankful Father let you come to see him off and that Anthony wanted you here."

"I am! But it is so hard, Lily. I don't know when I will see him again. Oh, how I wish to go with him as far as Queenstown."

"Don't be foolish," she chided softly.

The locomotive rumbled and suddenly the platform was a swirling ghost of steam. Flashes of colour and faces loomed in and out in an eerie fashion and the noise grated Lily's raw nerves. A harassed-looking porter pushing a trolley scurried behind an elderly gentleman and a crying child clutched the hand of his nanny, as he was half dragged towards the platform. Soon Anthony was swallowed up in the crowd.

All of a sudden, Josie cried out and pulled away, running towards the barrier. She pushed past the startled ticket collector and disappeared into the mêlée on the platform. Lily groaned, unsure if she should follow and drag her away. But minutes later, she spotted Anthony's tall figure. He was walking Josie back towards the barrier, his face set, obviously displeased. He said something to her, then gave her a gentle push. Josie slowly walked back towards her, tears streaming down her cheeks, shoulders slumped. Anthony stood stock-still at the barrier; but his eyes did not follow Josie — he was staring straight at her.

Dublin, 1918

Spanish Flu stalked Dublin's streets from the autumn of 1917 and Anthony's mother succumbed just after Christmas. Lily and her family attended her funeral in Glasnevin Cemetery and commiserated with Anthony's brother and sister. Josie confessed to Lily she hoped Mrs Lanigan's death would tempt Anthony home, but German U-Boats made the journey across the Atlantic a hazardous one. Only an extreme emergency would tempt anyone to make the journey since the sinking of the *Lusitania* only months after Anthony had left for America. Lily was secretly glad he had not ventured on such a risky course. She, too, was torn between longing to see him and fear for his safety.

More bad news followed in March when they received word that Will had been badly injured and was on his way to a convalescent hospital in England. It was while Father was making plans to travel to see him that Josie fell ill. The doctor believed it was influenza. For weeks she hovered between life and death and Lily and Margaret took turns to help nurse her as Mother was struggling to cope.

The priest was called one night and the family gathered and prayed together, clinging to each other for comfort. It seemed a miracle when days later she began to rally. By the end of the month, she was well enough to return to work and everyone sighed with heart-felt relief.

Some weeks later, Father paid an unexpected visit to the flat. Lily answered the door and knew immediately that something was amiss – he was deadly pale.

"What is it?" she asked. He sat down and stared at the floor, pulling at his gloves and swallowing hard. His silence scared her. Had one of those dreaded British Army telegrams arrived in North Earl Street? "Father? Is it Will?"

Margaret entered the room and stood silently behind him, giving her an anguished look.

"No, not Will. I found Josie doubled up this morning in the kitchen. You know she still has that awful cough?"

"Yes, I told her to go back to the doctor," Lily said.

"When she realised I was there she stuffed her handkerchief into her pocket, but not before I'd seen the blood."

"Lord, no!" Margaret said, her hand flying up to her mouth.

Lily's heart began to pound. It could only be tuberculosis. "Does Mother know?"

He swallowed hard. "No, I … I could not tell her. She is so worried about William's terrible injuries. It would break her."

"You must," she said. She knelt down beside him and took his hand. It was trembling. "And we must get Josie to the doctor."

"For all the good it will do!" Father said.

"We have to try," Margaret said with great determination. "There are sanatoriums, treatments – I'm sure something can be done for her."

Situated on a cliff, overlooking the sea, the sanatorium in Wicklow had plenty of the fresh air claimed to be beneficial to those who languished under the shadow of consumption. Lily and Margaret tried to visit Josie every Saturday afternoon after work. The grounds were beautifully maintained and when the weather was fine, they would often find Josie seated on a bench, beneath some pine trees, looking out to sea.

One particularly fine day, Lily visited alone and found Josie in her usual spot. They sat in companionable silence, enjoying the view, each lost in their own thoughts. Josie tucked her hand into hers and squeezed it.

"I like to look at the ocean," she said softly. "I know it's the wrong direction, but I try to imagine that Tony is just over the horizon." Her words cut Lily to the quick for she suspected for some time that his regard for Josie was waning.

Josie pulled an envelope from her pocket and handed it to her. "This arrived yesterday. See how hard he is working? Soon his plans will come to fruition and he will come home to me."

Lily's pulse quickened as she slid the letter from the envelope. The intervening years had not changed how she felt and just the thought of touching something from him gave her a guilty thrill. Over the years, Josie had let her read some of his letters. But reading down through this one, she was dismayed at its formality. There were no soft words or romance in it at all. He spoke of his recent promotion and continued success in his job, but there was no mention of coming home. She realised Josie was reading too much into his words.

"I'm sure as soon as the war is over he will return," she said, at last, straining to smile.

Josie's face lit up and she nodded. "I do hope so, Lily. I need him here," she said and dropped her head to rest it on her shoulder. Lily stared out to sea, her sister's wish echoing in her mind.

Peace was declared in November. It was too cold now for Josie to enjoy the grounds. Her ward, on the top floor, was bright and airy and looked out towards the mountains, bleak and beautiful in the late autumn light. Lily hated to see her there; she looked so small and frail in the bed. She had lost weight and had a sickly pallor to her skin. Her eyes were sunken and ringed with dark shadow.

Anthony's picture graced the bedside locker. It was a studio portrait of him sitting in a motor car with some friends. He smiled out from the photograph, looking healthy, prosperous and strong.

"It's safe now – when do you think he will come, Lily?"

"Soon, I'm sure, my dear," she answered. "Do not worry

about it. You must concentrate on getting better. You don't want him to see you here like this." Josie nodded and smiled before settling back in the bed as if a great weight had been lifted from her.

It was a few Sundays before Christmas and Lily was helping her mother in the kitchen after tea. Will, who had been discharged the week before was sitting with Father and Margaret in the parlour.

"He looks quite well, considering what he has been through," Lily said. Her mother didn't answer, but gripped the edge of the sink. "Mother, what is it?"

"What did they do to my poor boy?" she cried. "I can't bear it."

"Sit down and tell me," Lily pleaded. She helped her to a chair and waited, her heart pounding.

"I thought the worst thing would be his injuries, Lily. I was prepared for that but it is … he has changed."

"I imagine his experiences were dreadful and he has lost most of his leg."

Her mother shook her head. "No, Lily, it's not that. He hardly ever speaks – Will – the boisterous one who was always talking and laughing and singing. He sits in the parlour all day, morose and angry. He snaps at us if we try to talk to him. The nights are the worst. He has the most terrifying nightmares. He screams in his sleep." She started to cry.

Lily sat down and hugged her. "Oh Mother, why didn't you tell us? You know Margaret and I will do anything we can to help. Why don't I move back here for as long as you need me? Please don't be upset. You will make yourself unwell."

But with the war over, more and more injured men, some missing limbs, some disfigured, became a common sight on the city streets. Lily could not help but wonder what horrors were being relived behind the vacant eyes that met hers and slid away. The answer was at home. The bright and fun-loving brother who had left them almost four years before, was tortured by what he had endured and his vital spirit was broken. One evening, he eventually broke down and spoke of some of his experiences and the day he had been injured. She had to leave the room to weep.

When Lily and Father arrived, they were met at the front door of the sanatorium by Dr Grainger, the senior doctor.

"Would you mind coming to my office, please?" he asked. Her father looked at her with concern before they followed him. Dr Grainger ushered them into his office and shut the door.

"I'm sorry, Mr Cusack, it isn't good news. Your daughter's condition has deteriorated in the last week and is causing us some concern. It is only right that you be prepared for the worst," he said.

Lily gripped her father's arm, as much to steady herself as to support him. "How long, Dr Grainger?" she asked.

"I'm not sure. She may last until after Christmas," he said. He shrugged. "But it could be sooner."

"I'd like to see her now, please," her father said, his throat working.

"Of course. Would you like me to come with you?" the doctor asked.

"No, it's fine, thank you," Lily said and steered her father out of the room.

They walked slowly up the stairs to Josie's ward in absolute silence. When they reached the door, her father stalled. Lily began to panic. Josie would suspect something was wrong if Father didn't come in.

"We cannot tell her, Father," Lily warned.

"Yes, my dear, I know. It's just … this is so hard."

"Yes. Yes, it is," she said, before pushing open the door.

Josie was resting back against the pillows. Her eyes flew open as they approached and she smiled up at them.

"It must be Saturday," she whispered.

"Yes, dear," Lily said, bending down to kiss her forehead. "How are you feeling today?" Her skin was cool and clammy.

"Much better, Lily. If you look in the locker there is a new letter from Tony. One of the nurses read it for me. I do believe he will be home for Christmas. Isn't that wonderful?"

"Yes, love, that is the best news," Lily said, holding Josie's gaze while digging her fingers into her palms. Father winced and turned away.

"And Lily, he might bring me a present from America. What do you think it will be?"

"A fetching hat, or perhaps a nice little piece of jewellery?"

"I'd like that," Josie said. "I've always wanted a pearl brooch." Then she closed her eyes.

"Father?" Lily whispered, hoping he would say something comforting. He raised a shaking hand and walked away, pulling a handkerchief from his pocket before stumbling out the door.

Lily soon dreaded the journey each Saturday. Josie continued to decline and her spirits gradually sank. Lily found it heart-breaking to watch her crumble every time a male visitor appeared on the ward and passed by her bed. On New Year's Day, Josie finally admitted hope had deserted her. She turned her head to the wall and refused to speak to them anymore.

Christmas Eve, Dublin 1919
Christmas madness was upon the city. It was mid-morning and pedestrians were hurrying along North Earl Street, many laden down with parcels. Lily stood by the window. She searched among them for his familiar black fedora and distinctive gait. Perhaps he would look different. Would America have transformed how he looked or spoke? How strange that would be.

She had been privy to some of his letters to Josie. For the first year, they were full of wonder. Every experience had been described so vividly she could close her eyes and accompany him on his adventures. The excitement underpinning his words had left her longing to know more, but of course, she could not write to him. It would not have been proper while he was Josie's beau.

In the end, she was the one who had volunteered to undertake the dreadful task of informing him of Josie's passing. It had been the most difficult letter she had ever written. She had hesitated at the post box and stared at the address in Philadelphia. For a brief moment, she wished she could go and tell him in person. A letter felt such an impersonal way to deliver the news.

Anthony's response was addressed to her parents and Father later showed her the letter. Anthony's shock and distress were evident and she felt guilty for thinking he had stopped loving Josie. She grabbed her coat and escaped the house, hopping on the first tram that stopped. On the way out to Howth, she sat rigid with renewed grief. Alighting at the village, she walked down the West Pier, past courting couples and a few elderly matrons being pushed along in their bath chairs by their companions.

Halfway down, sheltering against the wind, she watched the fishermen unloading their catch. They called out cheerfully to each other, working steadily. Perhaps their weather-beaten faces held the answer. She, too, must find solace in her work and her family. That was all that mattered. She continued on to the end of the pier, fighting the urge to howl into the wind and let the tears fall. She had been a fool. He would never come back now – his life was in America and she must move on.

But now, five months later, she knew he was back in Dublin. He had sent a note to say he would visit them today. She took a deep breath and looked about the room which she had decorated for Christmas with holly, ivy and paper decorations. The overall effect was homely and welcoming. Father had trudged up the stairs with a small tree and she had done her best to cajole Will into helping her decorate it. He had given up after a few minutes, grumbling about his leg.

Lily often treated him to visits to the picture house or a coffee shop in an effort to distract him. But nothing seemed to please or interest him. His leg was a continual source of pain so he could not work for Father behind the counter downstairs or even do any heavy lifting. An artificial limb, courtesy of the British Army, had arrived the week before, but lay untouched in its box, behind his bedroom door.

On the mantelpiece, Josie's photograph smiled back at her. It was their best picture of her, taken on her seventeenth birthday. With her hair up and a crisp white dress, she looked quite the lady. Next to it was Margaret's wedding picture taken on the steps of the Procathedral and at the end was one of Will, looking resplendent in his uniform with Mother and Father either side of him. It had been taken the day he had left them for the theatre of war. She turned away, suddenly feeling impatient. Since Margaret's nuptials, she had moved back home, but her life had stood still for far too long. The resolutions she had made that day in Howth were unfulfilled.

"Come away from the window, Lily," Will snapped.

She took one last peep as an unfamiliar blue van pulled up outside. She could not make out the lettering on the side and with a sigh, she rejoined Will on the sofa. But he had buried his head in his book again and his defences were up. The ticking of the clock punctuated the silence. The waiting was killing her.

Then in the distance, she heard the jangle of the shop bell. She sat up straight and brushed down her skirts with nervous hands. She stayed perfectly still, straining to hear. He will have gone into the shop to see Father first, she thought. What possible excuse could she use to go down to the shop? She clasped her hands in her lap. You are a very foolish woman, she chided herself, and it may not even be Anthony down there at all. Then the front door gave its familiar creak and she heard Father's distinctive tread. But he entered the room alone. Where was Anthony? She held her breath.

"You have a rare treat in store, my dears," he said as Mother came in from the kitchen. "Just you wait and see."

Moments later Anthony was standing in the doorway, weighed down by an enormous package and grinning like a Cheshire cat. Father hurried to clear the table and Anthony gently placed the box down.

"Come and see," Father urged as he began to open the box. Lily slowly rose up, automatically putting out a hand to help Will. He brushed her aside and took up his walking stick and limped across the room ahead of her.

"It is good to see you again, Mrs Cusack," Anthony said, shaking Mother warmly by the hand.

"And you, Anthony," Mother answered, her voice full of emotion. "It has been too long."

"Indeed it has," he answered softly. He turned to Will. "It is good to see you, Will. I'm sorry for your trouble."

Will stiffened, but shook his hand. "Thank you, Anthony. Welcome home," he said.

Lily stepped forward. "It's good to see you again, Mr Lanigan."

As their hands touched, he smiled. His eyes held warmth and she could have sworn she felt a moment of pressure from his fingers.

"And you, Miss Cusack."

Just then Father and Mother exclaimed and Lily turned to see a Berliner gramophone emerge from the wrappings.

Will gasped. "It's the very latest – I've seen these in magazines. The sound quality is the very best"

Anthony smiled. "Yes, it is. This is a Christmas gift for you all. My new business venture – Lanigan Gramophones has just been born. I have brought crates full of these, and the latest records, back from America. There are some records here for you too," he said putting down a leather satchel and drawing them out. The records had beautiful colourful sleeves. Lily couldn't wait to see what they were.

"Here, Will, perhaps you would be good enough to set it up for me?"

Will beamed back at him. "Just try and stop me!"

Father took Anthony's arm. "So tell us all about your plans," he said, as he drew him towards the fireplace. "I'm intrigued."

"And you must stay and have lunch with us," Mother said.

"I'd be delighted, Mrs Cusack," he replied.

Lily caught the lightning glance he stole at her and felt her heart begin to pound. Unsure of herself, she stood near Will and pretended to be absorbed in what he was doing. As Anthony spoke to her parents, she studied him. He had barely changed. Only a faint twang in his voice told of his stint in America. She listened avidly as he told them about opening his shop on George's Street.

"In fact, I am in dire need of reliable help," he said, looking towards Will. "You wouldn't be interested, would you, Will? I hope to repair as well as sell them, you see, so I could train you up. What do you think?"

Will looked up, blushing. "I … well, I'm not sure that I would be able …"

"Of course you would," Mother said. "It would be the perfect job for you. You love music just as much as Anthony and you have always been handy. He was a radio operator during the war, you know," she continued. Will rolled his eyes but gave a lop-sided smile before returning to the job in hand.

Lily mouthed 'thank you' to Anthony and he smiled back.

"I say, have you got it working yet?" Anthony called over. "Mrs Cusack, would you care to choose a record?" He held out his arm and escorted her back to the table.

Mother sifted slowly through the selection and at last held one up. "Please, Anthony, I would love to hear this one."

"Will, set it up, there's a good man," Anthony said, with a wave of his hand.

Soon the opening chords of *The Blue Danube* drifted across the room.

"Ah, a waltz," Father exclaimed. "Perfect! Quick, Anthony – move those chairs back. It would be a shame not to take advantage." Much to her astonishment, Father winked at her.

Once a space had been cleared, Mother and Father started to waltz around the perimeter of the room. Will sat down beside the gramophone, a look of rapture on his face as he scrutinised the machine. Lily felt her throat tighten with gratitude and other emotions she could barely define.

The world suddenly felt right again.

Anthony walked up to her and held out his hand. "Would you do me the honour, Miss Cusack?"

"Please, call me Lily," she said, hoping her feet would remember how to move for she suddenly felt frozen to the spot.

"And you must call me Tony," he said, before taking her hand and leading her out in three-quarter time.

The End

The Lighthouse Keeper

"What a wonderful spot! How on earth did you find this place?" Sally asked, craning her neck to take in the full glory of the old lighthouse.

"Contacts, you know," Alex answered, with a wiggle of his eyebrows.

The building soared up into the sky, a huge black and white monument to man's belief he could conquer the elements. Sally was fascinated by lighthouses. Her father's painting of Hook Head had hung in pride of place over the fireplace back home in Ireland. Now a montage of lighthouse photos hung in the tiny bathroom of her London flat. Had Alex noticed? How clever and thoughtful of him.

The journey had been worth the hurried packing and the slow-moving traffic on the motorway. The country music he played in the car, however, was a whole different matter. But she was too polite to ask him to change it. She sighed; it could even be a deal-breaker. A lot hinged on this weekend.

He slammed the boot shut and came to stand beside her. "Here you go," he said, handing her the small overnight bag.

"I can't understand how you were able to book it – a bank holiday weekend, too. When I looked I could find nothing at all."

"Perhaps you didn't try hard enough," he said, ducking to avoid her badly aimed swipe. He laughed and moved towards the door. "Come on; let's get rid of these bags. I'm starving."

Sally took one last look at the towering structure then out to the calm sea beyond. A solitary seabird swooped and danced above the water and the gentle lapping of the waves on the shore below was a very pleasant sound. It was late afternoon and they had been in the car for over three hours. She longed for a walk along the shore, but it would have to wait. Alex was a pain when he was hungry.

He bent down and pulled a large bunch of keys from under a terracotta pot. "Ta-da!" he said. Whatever plant had called the pot home was now a soft brown mush. Sally wrinkled her nose at the smell of decay and pushed the container away. She hoped the interior was more promising, but had to wait as Alex battled with the lock and key. One final tug and the door swung open.

"Ladies first," he said, with a sweeping bow.

"Idiot!" she said, stepping over the threshold.

She shivered. The room, which appeared to be the kitchen, was absolutely freezing. The whitewashed walls did little to illuminate the room and one small narrow window was the only source of natural light. Sally flicked the wall switch. With a loud buzzing, the strip light jumped into life.

"I'll see if I can turn the heating on," Alex said and starting opening and closing cupboard doors.

"I think I spotted some outhouses around the corner," Sally said. "If there's a boiler, it must be in one of them."

"I didn't think we'd need to worry about heat in August," Alex grumbled and disappeared out the door.

At least it all looked reasonably clean, if a little old-fashioned. Sally began to relax. She wasn't given to acting on impulse, but when Alex had phoned her up and suggested a weekend away she couldn't resist. It was their first holiday together. A thrill of nervous excitement coursed through her veins. Sometimes she could not believe their relationship had lasted as long as it had for they were very different people from backgrounds worlds apart. His family were well-to-do while she came from a middle-class family from a small town in Ireland. They were still at that awkward stage of learning each other's foibles.

Sally pulled out her phone and wasn't too surprised to see there was no signal. Probably just as well, she thought and shoved it back into her handbag. She strolled around the room, pulling out drawers and opening cupboards. All the essentials were there. Would he expect her to play domestic goddess for the weekend, she wondered.

The window, which was above the sink, looked out to sea and in the distance she could make out the nearest headland and the treacherous rocks that snaked out into the water and gave the cove its deadly reputation. Black's Bay had been claiming seafaring lives for centuries. Naturally, she had googled the location as soon as Alex had told her where they were going. He had given her the task of booking the accommodation, but at such short notice, she had found nothing at all. But it was useful to have a boyfriend with connections. He had magically conjured up this place.

Curious now to see the rest, she made her way up to the next floor, winding her way up the metal steps that hugged the inner wall of the lighthouse. It was a lovely sitting room with old velvet-covered sofas and mismatched chairs. A jumble of what looked like second-hand furniture was scattered about. A dilapidated old stove dominated the room and someone had left a basket of logs. Sally smiled to herself; there were no radiators. Alex would not be pleased he had gone on a wild goose chase. She tried the sofa and found herself sinking down into it. Lovely. But there was more to see.

On the next level was the bedroom and bathroom and the final run of steps brought her to the old lamp room at the very top of the lighthouse. It had been converted at some stage and the old lantern and equipment were gone. A padded seat now ran around the perimeter, with a small table in the centre where a collection of sun-bleached books was scattered. Despite the ventilator in the roof, it was akin to standing in an oven for the glass storm panes with their metal supports formed a mini sunroom.

She tried the handle of the door out to the metal gallery which ran around the outside, as much to escape the heat as to give in to her curiosity. With a screech of ancient hinges, it swung open and she gingerly stepped out onto the platform. She stood mesmerised at the railing. The countryside and seascape stretched out for miles in every direction, a green and blue panorama, glowing in the afternoon sun. It felt as though she were looking down on a miniature world. The houses were small white rectangles, dotted along the coast road, on which a few cars moved, looking very much like toys.

"Ahoy!" she heard from down below.

"I'm up here – at the top," she called down.

Alex appeared at the top of the stairs, out of breath.

"What did you find?" she asked with a grin as he stepped out beside her.

"An outhouse full of equipment. I think it may have been the fog-warning set-up – all rusted up and covered in decades of dirt. No sign of a heating boiler," Alex said.

"There's a stove in the sitting room. It was probably too expensive or difficult to put in central heating."

He rolled his eyes and, to her surprise, he looked put out.

"Isn't it wonderful up here?" she said, hoping to distract him from his mood.

For a few moments, he took in the view. His blond hair rippled in the breeze and she longed to run her hand through it, but felt too shy to act. He turned to her, his face transformed. "Bloody marvellous!" He reached across and drew her into his arms. "Not quite as marvellous as you, though," he murmured, kissing her soundly.

Some minutes later they came up for air.

"Glad you came?" he asked, his eyes soft with desire.

"Oh well, you know, I was at a loose end anyway."

He chuckled. "Are all Irish girls as elusive as you?"

"Of course – it's hard-wired into our DNA," she said. She stepped out of his embrace and moved further along the gallery. "I wonder what it was like to live and work here."

"Cold, as we have just discovered, and smelly! They used

kerosene in the lamps back in the day. I imagine it was hard work and always on the night shift. I don't think I would have liked it. Despite the wonderful views, I prefer my nice comfy Canary Wharf office," Alex said. "I suppose it appeals to your romantic soul?"

She looked at him, unsure if he was being sarcastic. "I grew up by the sea and I do miss it. Someday I hope to again."

"I admit having a weekend place does appeal to me, but maybe not a freezing lighthouse. Come on, let's head back to town. I could eat my own arm at this stage."

Relieved he didn't expect her to cook, she took one last look out to sea before following him back inside.

It was well past midnight as they drove back along the coast road. A full moon hung in the sky casting a faint glow over the landscape. Sally watched the silhouette of the lighthouse materialise, its shape so distinctive against the silvery sea.

"It's a little eerie, don't you think?" Alex said. "Especially with that moon."

"No, it's wonderful," she said, "almost Gothic."

"We will have to do something about your taste in reading material," he said, with a sideways glance as they pulled up outside the lighthouse. She grimaced into the darkness; it didn't sound like he was joking.

"Lord, this place is so cold," Alex said on opening the front door.

"Yes," she agreed, shivering. "It's warmer outside. Maybe it's because of the thickness of the walls."

"Yes, but why rent the place out if you aren't going to invest in the basics? They should have warned me about the heating. There's little point in firing up the stove this late."

"Was it particularly cheap?" she asked, as she pulled off her jacket.

"What's that supposed to mean?" he snapped, turning and glaring at her.

"Well if it was, the lack of facilities might be the reason," she pointed out in what she considered a reasonable tone. He grunted and headed up the stairs.

She stared after him. He was showing a different side this evening; she had never known him to be so tetchy. She sighed and was suddenly hit by a wave of nausea. She clutched her stomach as a spasm of cramp took her breath away. Once it had passed she grabbed a chair and sat down, breathing in shallow gasps. A radio was turned on upstairs and she heard the clink of a glass. She leant her head back against the wall, the top rail of the chair biting into the back of her shoulders. Closing her eyes, she listened to the song and willed her stomach to settle down.

Ice-cold fingers suddenly touched her cheek. She gasped, her eyes flying open and her heart racing. She jumped to her feet, knocking over the chair. Frantically, she scanned the room. There was no one there.

"What are you doing down there?" Alex called out.

"Coming," she said, breathing hard. She picked up the chair with trembling hands, all her senses on high alert. She stood still and tried to slow her breathing. The only sound in the kitchen was the buzzing of the strip light and the ticking of the wall clock. Whatever had upset her tummy was playing tricks on her mind, too. There was no other explanation. Feeling rather foolish, she climbed the stairs to join Alex.

He was lounging on the sofa, eyes closed, glass of whisky in his hand. His eyes opened as she approached. "Want one?" he asked, his voice slightly slurred. She didn't think he had drunk that much at dinner, but he looked half-cut now.

"Is there any brandy? My tummy is a bit off," she said. She needed it more for her nerves, but she wasn't going to tell him about what had just happened. He would only laugh.

Alex jerked his head towards the cabinet on the far side of the room. "Help yourself," he said. She looked at him in disgust, before rooting around in the cabinet. At the back, she found a dusty bottle of Hennessy.

"Is this some kind of ruse to get out of going sailing

tomorrow?" he asked. "I really want to go. I couldn't believe my luck seeing Doug Hatchet in the restaurant. A useful man to know. There is no way I'm going to pass up on an opportunity like that."

"I haven't asked you to," she said, gripping the bottle of brandy tightly, willing herself not to react. "Let's see how I am in the morning. Hopefully, it's nothing."

"Well, there's nothing wrong with me and we ate the same things," he said, his voice verging on a whine.

"No, I had the prawn starter. I think it might have been that."

She took her glass and sat down in one of the chairs opposite Alex. He was now half sprawled on the sofa and seemed barely aware of her presence. She downed the contents of her glass, grateful for the burning sensation of the alcohol hitting the back of her throat and the slow release of warmth relaxing the knots in her stomach.

Why did he have to be such a handsome pig, she wondered with a reluctant smile. Despite his inebriated state and foul humour she couldn't help but like him. It had been instant attraction for her; not just because he was tall, broad-shouldered with a winning smile that leapt into his cobalt-blue eyes. He was well-educated, intelligent and, on the first few dates, had been utterly charming. Had it all been show? Was this the real Alex?

A wave of disappointment swept over her. Since moving to London, two years before, she had despaired of ever finding love. A string of uninspiring dates had left her disillusioned. She had thrown herself into her work at the gallery, determined to focus on her career. The day she had met Alex, she had just been told she was being promoted. It was as if all the planets had suddenly come into alignment.

"I'm off to bed," she said. The only answer was a snore.

She lay rigid, her heart thumping. There it was again; a cranking sound, followed by footsteps on the floor above. The bedroom was almost in complete darkness but for the twisted shadow of the metal steps visible on the far wall. Alex must have left the light on downstairs in the sitting room. She groped for her phone on the locker. It was ten past two. She felt the sheet on the other side of the bed. It was cold. What on earth was he doing up in the lamp room?

A loud snore broke the silence, but it came from the sitting room. That didn't make any sense. Was she half asleep and dreaming the rest? When she found the switch for the bedside lamp, she flicked it on. She pushed back the duvet and gasped when her foot touched the icy floorboard. Grabbing her jumper, she pulled it over her head and went halfway down the steps into the sitting room. Sure enough, he was sound asleep where she had left him, a throw half covering his slumbering form. It seemed cruel to wake him.

She went back upstairs, disgruntled, and jumped under the duvet, jumper and all. She couldn't stop shaking. Her imagination was playing tricks. Strange place, strange bed – that would account for it. For all of it.

She turned off the light, thumped her pillow and tried to subdue her disappointment. So much for romance, she thought. Why had she bothered sacrificing her lunch hour, the previous day, to get her hair done, legs waxed and buy new underwear? She felt a fool. He was more interested in his proposed sailing trip tomorrow. Still; better to find out what he is like now. She made up her mind that she would not go with him tomorrow even if she felt better. She would drive into town and spend a pleasant hour or two strolling around the quaint streets that led up from the harbour. There might even be a nice little gallery to explore.

As the sleepless minutes slipped by, she became aware of the wind picking up; a lonely plaintive sound, making her uneasy. No wonder her mind was playing tricks. From now on she would stick to admiring lighthouses from the outside.

The floorboards above creaked. Then there were footsteps and the sound of something being dragged across the floor.

Suddenly her body was humming with adrenaline and she broke out in a cold sweat. Her senses were straining and all at once the overpowering smell of kerosene pervaded the room. Terrified, she could not move. The sound of metal scraping against metal sent a shiver down her spine. To her horror, as she watched, a powerful beam of light flitted across the opening to the upper level. Impossible, a voice inside her head said, but there it was again: a sweep of light that lit the room with an intensity that hurt her eyes.

She bolted from the bed. Almost tripping down the steps in her haste, she lunged at Alex where he lay.

"Wake up!" she shouted at him, shaking his arm.

Alex groaned and slowly opened his eyes. He stared at her, coughed and ran his fingers through his hair. "What the hell, Sally? I was fast asleep."

"The lighthouse is working – there is someone up there!" she whispered.

"Don't be daft, Sal. This place was decommissioned years ago," Alex said, sitting up. He stretched his arms over his head and yawned. "You must have had a nightmare," he said, getting to his feet.

"I did not imagine it, Alex. I heard footsteps and noises, strange noises. Then I saw a beam of light."

Alex shook his head, then suddenly grinned. "Must have been those prawns, eh?"

Sally knew it was a lost cause; he would never believe her. She tried to smile. "Maybe."

"Bed – come on," he said, pushing her towards the stairs.

"No! You go first," she said, hanging back.

Alex scowled. "This is ridiculous, Sally." He went up and disappeared from view. She followed very slowly indeed.

Sally stood at the door and watched Doug Hatchet's Aston Martin drive away. Alex didn't even wave; she knew he was miffed that she wouldn't go with them. Over breakfast, he had convinced her the previous night's excitement had been down to a nightmare. A tiny part of her wasn't so sure. Of course in daylight everything appeared to be normal and almost to prove she wasn't afraid, she took her second cup of strong coffee up to the lamp room.

She sat looking out to sea. The glorious sunshine of the previous day was gone and a bank of ominous clouds brooded on the horizon. The wind, which had unsettled her during the night, had strengthened and whistled around the building as if searching for cracks and gaps in its structure. She had mentioned it to the men, but they had laughed and dismissed her concerns, leaving her feeling rather foolish.

Inside the lighthouse, all was quiet. Whatever presence she had sensed the night before was gone. No; it was never there. She was being foolish. The real issue was Alex's behaviour. That and the strangeness of the old building were affecting her.

It wasn't in her nature to mope. She would enjoy a leisurely day. Alex was unlikely to be back before six. She was glad he was gone, for now she could explore the beach below at her own pace, drive into town for her lunch and investigate all of the quaint shops she had spied on passing through the day before. Decision made, she felt better.

It was only ten-thirty and the beach was almost deserted except for a few dog walkers and solitary strollers. The other bank holiday visitors were probably still in bed. She could not understand why anyone would come all this way, to such a beautiful place, and waste their time indoors. She set off at a brisk pace, facing the wind and enjoying the magnificent views and the tangy scent of the ocean. It was wonderful to be back on a beach and the wilder the weather, the more exhilarating it was. The sand dunes towered above the strand to the west, moulded by the wind and the sea, and the marram grasses swayed back and forth like graceful ballerinas pirouetting in the wind.

Up close it wasn't difficult to see why the bay was so

dangerous, for, at intervals along the shore, jagged fingers of shiny black rock protruded out into the water only to disappear and lurk beneath the waves. She stood and watched the foaming sea horses pound the rocks and she could feel the spray dampening her face as it drifted on the wind. She closed her eyes and let her senses roam free. She felt at peace. A dog raced past her chasing a ball and broke the spell. With some reluctance, she moved on.

About halfway towards the far headland she felt the first few drops of rain. Disappointed, she turned, hoping she could make it back to the lighthouse before it got any heavier. With surprise, she saw that she was alone on the beach. So absorbed in her own thoughts she had not seen the signs of the approaching weather. She happened to look up and stopped dead. A prickle of fear made her catch her breath. There was someone up in the lamp room of the lighthouse, but it was too far away to tell who it was. The shape moved; a tall figure in dark clothes. It *must* be Alex. The sailing trip must have been cancelled. He was probably looking for her. She broke into a run.

By the time she reached the lighthouse door, she was soaked through. She fumbled with the key.

"Alex?" she called out on entering the kitchen. No reply.

She continued to call him as she went up through the building. Surely he could hear her now? She stepped out into the lamp room. To her astonishment, it was empty. The outside gallery was deserted. There was no one in the lighthouse.

Just her. Alone.

The wind and rain lashed against the panes of glass. A fully fledged storm was raging outside now. She tried to stay calm and make sense of it. Who had she seen if not Alex? It must have been a shadow – a trick of the light from the multitude of panes of glass. But where *was* Alex? They had hardly gone out sailing if the storm had been forecast? Alex said Doug was an experienced sailor. But what if the wonderful Doug hadn't checked the forecast? She had disliked him on sight the previous evening. Fifty-something and full of arrogant swagger, he was exactly the kind of man she would avoid at all costs.

Suddenly anxious, she knelt on the seat and tried to see through the driving rain. It was impossible. Everything was grey; sky and sea and beach. Feeling isolated, she began to panic. She pulled her phone out of her bag. Not one bar of signal showed. Damn.

There was nothing for it but to go into town and check at the harbour. Hopefully, the two men were ensconced in the yacht club bar. The possibility that they were out in that storm was just too awful to contemplate. She swiftly changed her clothes, towelled her hair and pulled it into a ponytail. She made a cursory effort to fix her make-up and she was ready to go. Just as she grabbed Alex's car keys from the kitchen table, she caught the movement of a dark shape at the bottom of the stairs. The faint whiff of kerosene stung her nostrils and the hairs on the back of her neck stood up. Without a backwards glance, she slammed the door and raced to the car.

"Was it not to your liking, miss?" the man asked. Sally looked up. The middle-aged waiter gave her an apologetic smile and gestured towards the table. "You've hardly touched the soup."

Sally looked down at the cold tomato soup then back to the man. "I ... I'm not particularly hungry."

"Shall I take it away then?"

She nodded and resumed her vigil. For the last hour and a half, she had been sitting at the window table of the cafe, watching the harbour for any sign of life. The rain-drenched streets were deserted and most of the shops had shut. She checked her phone again. No missed calls. No texts. Surely he must realise she would be worried.

The man cleared his throat. "Excuse me, but is something the matter?"

"I'm waiting for a friend. He went sailing earlier with a mate of his."

"Good grief! They went out in that?" the man exclaimed, sounding concerned. He looked out towards the sea and grimaced.

"I'm afraid so," she said with an attempt at a smile. A sudden gust of wind drove the rain hard against the window. She trembled and pulled her jacket tighter around her body.

The man shifted uncomfortably, his friendly face marred by a frown. "Very foolish to go out on a day like this. Those storms get up very suddenly along this stretch of coast. The locals know, but it's easy for tourists to get caught out."

Sally felt her stomach turn. "Do you think I should inform the coastguard?"

He bit his lip. "What time did they go out?"

"First thing," she said.

"Of course they may have taken shelter further up the coast. Do you know which way they were heading?"

"No," she said. "But I don't think they planned to go too far."

"Does he have his phone with him?"

Her eyes strayed to her silent phone. "Yes, but there is no answer. It's going to voicemail."

"Perhaps, just to be on the safe side, we should make that call," he said.

Sally stood anxiously at the counter as he dialled and asked for the coastguard. She fed him the details when asked.

"You could do with a strong cup of tea," he said when he hung up. "I'm Frank, by the way," he said, holding out his hand. "The owner of this fine establishment."

"Sally O'Connor," she said, suddenly grateful for Frank's firm handshake and bonhomie; she had a feeling she might need serious cheering up. "I think I'll take you up on that offer of tea. Thank you, Frank."

Past Imperfect

"Go on over to the table. I'll only be a jiffy."

As she sat down and peered out the window, she heard Frank talking quietly to his assistant. The only other customers, an elderly couple, got up and paid. As they left, a blast of rain-laden wind whooshed through the door. Frank had to spring forward to close it after them. There was no let-up; it was torrential. She could only imagine how high the sea must be.

"There we go," Frank said a few minutes later, placing a steaming cup before her. "Don't you be worrying. I'm sure they will have taken shelter somewhere. Quite an adventure he's had today – something to impress his mates with in the pub, for years to come." He slid into the seat opposite.

Sally nodded half-heartedly. It was kind of him to try and cheer her up, but she had a horrible sick feeling in her stomach. Something was very wrong.

"Are you just here for the weekend?" he asked.

"Yes, we are staying out at Black's Bay."

"One of those nice holiday homes, eh? They are very popular. Mike Ainsley made a killing developing those. Hardly ever empty, in fact. Not that I'm complaining, mind you. It's good for my business, too."

"No – there was no availability. Alex arranged for us to stay at the lighthouse."

"Oh!" Frank exclaimed, paling visibly. "I … didn't think it was let out anymore."

"Why did you say 'oh' like that?"

"No reason," he said, suddenly very interested in the road outside.

"Is there something I should know?" she probed.

Frank flicked his gaze around the room and lowered his voice. "That place has a bad history, that's all. Hard to know what's fact and what's fiction. I'm sure it's fine for a night or two."

"But you wouldn't stay in it. Am I right?" she asked, half fearing her concerns were about to be confirmed.

36

"It has a bit of a reputation," he said.

"For what, exactly? Why not tell me about it – it will take my mind off Alex," she suggested, with an anguished glance out the window as a huge wave came over the harbour wall.

"Ah, you know how these things get blown out of proportion; silly folks saying things when they have had a few drinks."

Sally tilted her head. "Please."

Frank sat back in his chair and sighed. "OK, if you insist. The lighthouse was decommissioned in the early 1890s. There was an incident in Black's Bay. A ship went aground and many on board lost their life. It was said the lighthouse keeper fell asleep on the job and the lamp went out. It was around the time the electric came in. They closed it all down after that and built a more modern beacon on the next headland."

"What happened to the poor lighthouse keeper? I assume he lost his job."

"Well, it was said that his wife was on board the ship that went down. He threw himself from the lighthouse gallery when he found out."

"My God! The poor man!"

"Yes, indeed. It was an awful tragedy. It is claimed that … some say he never left. On stormy nights people have sworn they have seen the light sweeping the bay. People reckon his ghost is trying to warn sailors of the danger."

Sally felt her blood run cold.

"Are you all right? You've gone very white," Frank said, leaning towards her.

Sally let out a slow breath. "I thought I saw and heard something last night, but I'm fairly sure it was a bad dream."

Frank nodded, but looked at her with a strange expression. "Of course it was; there's no such thing as ghosts." He didn't sound very convinced.

Sally parked up outside the lighthouse. Dusk was falling and still there was no word from the coastguard or the police.

Frank had taken her number and promised to call if he heard anything. The keys to the lighthouse were on the passenger seat. Every so often she picked them up and contemplated going inside, only to change her mind. What was waiting for her in there?

Her heart leapt when her phone buzzed. "Hello? Alex?" she said, gripping the phone tightly.

"Who's Alex? Is that your new chap?" It was her father.

"Oh, Dad, it's you," she said.

"Sorry to disappoint you," he said.

"No, no; sorry, Dad. I'm in a bit of bother – I'm really glad you rang." She explained what had happened as briefly as she could.

"Do you want me to come over? I could catch a flight first thing."

"No, Dad. I can't ask you to do that; you have Mum to look after," she said. "I'm sure he'll turn up soon."

"I hope so, love. But just say the word, and I'll hop on a plane. Your Aunt Mary will come and look after Mum."

"Really, there is no need."

"Have you eaten?" he asked.

"No, I couldn't."

"Go inside and make yourself something to eat and a stiff drink mightn't go amiss. As for all the strange stuff – don't be afraid, love. Old buildings can be very creepy, especially at night. How many times did I tell you when you were a child that you had an overactive imagination?"

"I know what I saw and heard, Dad. I didn't imagine it."

This was greeted by silence. He cleared his throat. "All you can do is wait. Promise me you'll look after yourself. Ring me if there is any news."

"I will, Dad. Thanks."

She stared at the dead phone for several minutes, willing it to ring again; hoping it would be Alex. There was no signal inside but she couldn't sit in the car all night either. "This is daft," she said out loud. "I'm going in."

After devouring hastily made scrambled eggs, and with the universal panacea for all ills clutched in her hand, she made her way up to the sitting room. As she sat sipping her tea, she noticed the wind had dropped. The storm had moved away and the lighthouse was cloaked in silence. Uncomfortable silence. She fiddled about with the radio as the channel Alex had set was, predictably enough, a country music one. Ella Fitzgerald's velvety tones were far preferable. She settled back down, wrapped herself in the throw and started to feel the tension easing from her muscles. Five minutes later, she was fast asleep.

She jolted awake and lay for several seconds confused and edgy. The room felt icy-cold. Shaking her head, she eased into a sitting position. Then she saw him.

Alex. Sitting opposite her in one of the old armchairs.

Stunned, she could only stare at him. Then she noticed he was wet, soaking wet. A dark puddle had formed on the floor at his feet. His head was in his hands and he was trembling.

She sat forward, her body tense. "My God, Alex! What happened? Where have you been? I've been so worried."

He raised his head and looked at her with red-rimmed eyes. "I'm so sorry. I've let you down."

"No, please; I'm just glad you're safe. You're wringing wet – you must change before you catch pneumonia." He rose up from the chair. "Do you need any help?"

He shook his head and slowly climbed the stairs.

Sally raced down to the kitchen and put the kettle on; a hot whisky would help him feel more the thing. How had he got back? Had the coastguard brought him? She'd forgotten to ask about his friend. As she waited for the kettle to boil, she listened intently, but she could not hear him. The radio was still on.

Once it had boiled, she grabbed the kettle and brought it upstairs. "I'm making you a hot toddy, Alex. Come down as soon as you are ready," she called up.

She mixed the drink and waited patiently. Five minutes,

ten minutes – what was keeping him? Eventually, her patience ran out and up she went. He wasn't in the bedroom and the bathroom was in darkness. As she turned she saw the wet footprints on the floor leading over to the stairs. She stood uncertain at the bottom, looking up into the lamp room. Why on earth would he go up there now?

The metal rail was icy cold to the touch as she ascended. The lamp room was in darkness and it was empty.

Bewildered, she twirled around

Nothing.

The gallery was empty, too.

He had vanished.

It was then she remembered the front door was locked and the key was in her pocket.

One Month Later

Sally stood at her flat window and looked out across the rooftops. In the distance, she could make out the park where the treetops showed the first fiery touch of autumn. They had met in that park, sheltering under the same coppice of beech trees during a brief but heavy shower. With his blond good looks and upper-class accent, she had been astonished when Alex Vine had chatted her up. The following weekend they had gone out on their first date. Was it really only three months ago?

Since Alex's disappearance, she had found it very difficult to concentrate on anything. Her boss had made comments at work. Her friends had stopped mentioning him. Even her dad was avoiding the subject. She had felt awkward and unwanted at the memorial service. His family had been polite but distant. Somehow they seemed to think it was her fault. Sometimes she thought it, too. Why hadn't she talked him out of the stupid sailing trip?

Her thoughts were interrupted by the sound of the letter box. A large envelope lay on the hall floor and she recognised her father's handwriting. Pulling it open, she went back into the sitting room. A brief note and an old book slid out into her hand.

Dearest Sal, found this old local history of Black's Bay on Amazon. Thought you might find it of interest.

Talk soon,

Dad.

She turned over the book: *The Curse of Black's Bay*, by Charles Ainsley. She put it down with distaste. Black's Bay was the last place she wanted to hear about.

Her phone buzzed. Picking it up she hesitated for a moment as she didn't recognise the number.

"Hello?" she said.

"Is that Sally?" a vaguely familiar voice asked.

"Yes, it is. Who is this?"

"Frank. You might remember me from a few weeks back? You were the lady whose friend went missing – you were in my cafe."

Sally's heart sank. "Oh yes, hello, Frank." She remembered leaving her card with him on that awful Saturday evening.

"I'm sorry to bother you, but I thought you'd like to know the news now rather than read about it in the newspaper. The boat was found earlier today – they brought it in about an hour ago. It was smashed up pretty bad."

"Did ... did they find them?"

"Yes, I'm afraid so. I'm very sorry."

She closed her eyes, squeezing them tight. The tiny hope that he was still alive somewhere was dashed.

Alex was truly gone.

"Are you still there?" he asked.

"Yes. I'm sorry I have to go," she said, cutting off the call. She dropped the phone and sat down at the table, staring at the pattern of flowers on the oilcloth covering. She wanted to cry, but felt only numbness. She reached for the phone, then froze. His family would have been informed by the coastguard or the police. They would not want to hear from her, of all people. Well, no matter; she would go to the funeral and say goodbye properly. She owed him that.

It was the day after the funeral. Much to her relief, her father had accompanied her to the service. It had been as awful as she had feared. Having thoroughly dissected it all, they sat over the remains of their breakfast.

"Did you ever read that book I sent you?" her father asked. "If you are finished with it, I wouldn't mind reading it. I thought it looked quite interesting."

"I'm sorry; I just couldn't bring myself to look at it."

"Ok, love, I can understand that," he said with a gentle smile.

"I'm not sure where it is. I promise I'll look for it and bring it home with me next week."

Later that afternoon, after seeing her father off, Sally looked around the sitting room, trying to remember where she had put the blasted book. She eventually found it pushed to the back of the bookcase. She pulled it out, running her hand over the wine-coloured leather binding. Only it was her dad who had bought it, she would have thrown it in the bin. With a sigh, she opened it and reluctantly began to read. Within minutes she was transported back to the lighthouse on Black's Bay. It made for bleak reading. Over the centuries, countless souls had been lost at sea so tragically close to land. The strangely-shaped rocks she had seen on the beach were known locally as Black's Fingers, and were the cause of all the trouble, as they lay in wait beneath the water for any unsuspecting sailor.

Eventually, a group of local gentry had paid for the erection of the lighthouse and employed a local man as keeper. Jonas Armstrong kept the lamp lit and was heralded as a hero by the locals. It was reckoned his dedication to his duty had saved countless lives. Until one night, after three days and nights of high winds and stormy seas, during which he had valiantly manned the light, he succumbed to exhaustion. The light went out. In the bay below, the ship bearing his wife and son ran aground on the rocks and only a handful survived. As the cafe owner had recounted, Jonas was so distressed on learning the news, he threw himself to his death from the lighthouse, onto the rocks below, where his body was found the next day.

Several more pages told of suspected sightings of Jonas or the beam of light, in the intervening years, particularly just before a storm. A family photograph of the Armstrong family was included, dated 1887. Sally stared at the picture for some time. A wave of sadness swept over her as she thought about how their lives had ended so tragically. The stiff formality of their pose conveyed very little unless, of course, you knew their history.

The last few pages were an appendix; a chronological list of those who lost their lives in Black's Bay. Sally sifted through the pages, noting some of the names and dates. When she reached the last page she stared at it in disbelief. Before her eyes, two faint entries began to appear.

Her disbelief turned to horror as the name Douglas Hatchet began to form as if an invisible hand was at work.

With agonising slowness, the last entry appeared.

Alex Vine, aged 32, claimed by the sea, August 2016.

The End

The Promise

Winter, Ireland, 1912

Maura Hegarty looked up with a start as the wind rattled the windows. She hated stormy nights particularly when her father was still out and about. Flexing her aching shoulder muscles, she shifted in her seat and leaned closer to the oil lamp. Her fingers hurt, but she had to finish the embroidery on her veil. If only she had chosen a simpler design, but when her sister Róisín had shown her the picture in the magazine she had fallen in love with it. Rose-buds and tiny birds. Perfect. Ruefully, she glanced at the bundle of fabric on the table. She still had the intricate lace collar of her dress to finish.

The front door opened and the delicate netting of the sheer white veil fluttered in the disturbed air. It was her father, at last. She looked up and gave him a warm smile as he dragged off his boots and left them by the door.

He looked utterly exhausted. Ever since young William from the farm next door had left for Dublin, he had no help at all with the heavy work. The strain was starting to show on his craggy features. She put aside her sewing.

"Sit down, Father. I'll fetch your dinner."

"Thank you, my dear. I'll miss you when you get wed, you know." He sat down with a sigh.

Maura smiled and touched his shoulder. "Sure, I'll only be up the road and I promise to drop in your dinner every other day. Róisín's happy to do the same. Between the two of us, you'll not starve."

"I must have the best daughters in Ireland."

She placed the steaming plate of food in front of him. He

sniffed delightedly and grinned up at her. Maura took the seat beside him. "Any news? Did you see anyone today?"

Her father gave her a sly look followed by one of his roguish grins. "I might have."

"Who? Do tell. I've been stuck in all day."

"I met Patrick's father down by the lake."

Maura grabbed his arm. "Has he heard from him? Has he set sail yet?"

Her father chewed for a moment. "Would you believe they got a letter from him this very morning?"

"And?" Maura asked breathlessly.

"It's good news. He's due home in about a week, my dear. Now, you can stop your worrying."

Maura could not help smiling. Thank goodness Patrick was on his way. She hadn't seen him in almost a year. His letters from New York had been infrequent of late, but she knew he wasn't much of a one for writing. Róisín said some uncomplimentary things about it and they had fallen out for a brief time. But Maura knew him better and loved him fiercely. Her only fear had been he would wait too long and get caught up in the winter storms on the Atlantic. He had to be home on time; the banns were read, and the church was booked for the end of the month. First thing, she would go down to Fr Murphy and tell him the good news.

Next morning, just as Maura prepared to leave the house, there was a gentle tap-tap at the door. Mrs Brookfield, their elderly landlady who lived in the big house out at the lake, stood on the threshold, a parcel tucked under her arm. Maura could see her pony and trap in the yard.

"Good morning to you, Maura. I hoped I'd catch you in," she said.

"Please come in, Mrs Brookfield," Maura said taking a surreptitious peek at the clock as she pulled back the door; she wanted to catch Fr Murphy after mass. Hopefully, Mrs Brookfield wouldn't stay too long but she had to be polite.

"My father is out on the land, I'm afraid he won't be back until dinner."

"No, child, don't worry. It's you I've come to see."

Maura was surprised. "Would you like a cup of tea, ma'am?"

"Not at all, my dear. I've just come to give you this," Mrs Brookfield said, laying the parcel down on the scrubbed kitchen table. "'Tis a wedding present for you and Mr Maguire."

"How kind!" exclaimed Maura, itching to know what was inside the perfectly wrapped brown paper.

"I doubt anyone else has given you one of these," the lady said, taking a seat. "Go on! Open it."

She felt guilty. She should wait until Patrick was home and they could open their wedding gifts together. But, as she had already opened every other gift, it hardly mattered. She carefully untied the string and pulled back the paper, careful not to tear it so it could be reused. Inside was a crisp linen tablecloth, so white it almost glowed. Maura sucked in her breath. "Mrs Brookfield, it's beautiful. Thank you so much."

"Ah now, don't you deserve it, child, and you looking after your father these five years since your dear mother passed. It's your turn for a little happiness. Patrick Maguire comes from a good family. I'm pleased for you."

"I don't know how to thank you," Maura said, her eyes welling up.

"No need at all, my dear … but I might have that cup of tea after all and you can show me your progress with your trousseau."

As Maura left the sacristy and made her way down the side of the church, she heard her name being called. Róisín was waiting for her at the front gate, a smile on her pretty face.

"I heard the news about Patrick," Róisín greeted her as she drew up beside her. "Full steam ahead, now."

"Nothing stays secret around here," Maura said, linking

her arm as they walked slowly along the road towards home.

"Why would it be a secret from your own sister, pray? Anyway, isn't it about time he showed his face back here?"

Maura scowled at her but only for a moment; she was unable to contain her growing excitement.

"Róisín, I'm so happy! He'll be home in about a week. I hope he is pleased with everything I've arranged for the wedding. It hasn't been easy making all the decisions on my own."

"It will be splendid. Sure it's to be the wedding of the season," Róisín said in a grand la-de-dah voice.

Maura smiled. "Don't be silly." But she was pleased all the same.

"He doesn't deserve you."

"Don't start that again, Róisín."

"Those Maguire's look down on everyone else. My Edward had another run-in with Pat Senior."

"Ah Róisín, not again!" The Maguire land ran next to Edward's. "What was it this time?"

"Our sheep strayed on to their land again. I don't know what the fuss is about. Sure isn't it a big enough mountain and plenty of grazing for everyone's animals? Maguire is never happy unless he is complaining about something or other."

"They've been very kind to me," Maura said.

"That might have something to do with Father promising your Patrick the lease of the farm when he's gone. Why else would they accept you with such a small dowry?"

"Patrick and I love each other. The dowry made no difference to him. Besides, Mrs Brookfield is happy for Patrick to take on the lease. The arrangement suits everybody."

Roisin sniffed. "Old Pat is the most cunning man in the district. Didn't he get his own daughter off his hands for little or nothing. He's a mean auld fella. Everyone says it."

Maura stood still. "I did hear it and I don't believe a word of it. That was all idle gossip. It's a love-match, just like mine." She pulled her scarf closer around her neck, feeling chilly all of a sudden. "I just wish you could be happy for me. You found a great man in Edward. Why would you begrudge me the same?"

"I don't … I just don't want to see you get hurt. As your big sister, I have to look out for you."

Maura smothered her stinging reply. With only a few weeks to the wedding, and so much to do, she didn't want to fall out with her sister again.

The weather had been foul all week but a determined Maura made her way down the mucky boreen which led to the Maguire house. She was so nervous she'd had trouble buttoning up her coat before she left home and her father's teasing hadn't helped. Would Patrick have changed, she wondered. Did he still love her? As she neared the house, her nerves began to jangle. She could hear laughter coming from the house. Patrick always made people laugh. She quickened her step. God, she had missed him so much. She was dying to see him again.

Mrs Maguire opened the door and welcomed her in, taking her coat and shooing her towards the small parlour. As she entered the room, her senses were overpowered by the fumes of whisky and cigarettes. Momentarily self-conscious, she scanned the room for his familiar face. There he was. Standing before the fireplace, he was holding forth, his audience in rapt attention.

"'Tis Maura!" interrupted one of his younger brothers and everyone turned to look at her. Patrick turned too and she could have sworn she saw a flicker of annoyance cross his face before he smiled.

Pat Senior rose from his seat and offered it to her. "You're just in time, Maura. Patrick is telling us all about New York and how grand it is."

Patrick linked her arm as they made their way towards the road in the darkness. The rain had stopped at last. Maura stole a glance up at his profile, barely visible but for the weak light from the lantern he carried. Still the same hooked nose and strong chin. But there was something different about him. She wasn't sure what it was. It made her uneasy.

"Before I forget, Patrick, Fr Murphy wants to see you," she said.

"For what?"

Maura frowned into the darkness. "To talk about the big day, of course."

"Oh, yes." Patrick drew to a halt. "We should have a chat about all of that. I've been thinking, maybe we should wait until the spring."

"But the banns have been read. I've a heap of presents in my bedroom. Wait till you see them, Patrick. People have been so kind."

"Aye. Well, it's just all happening so quickly," he said, looking off into the distance. "Going to America has opened my eyes, Maura. There is such a big world out there. New York is a fine place. So modern. It's made me realise there has to be more than this old place. People are so backward here."

Maura smarted. "Including me?"

"No, no, I mean the old folk. Sure, you know it too. It's suffocating."

"I love living here. I thought it was all settled. My father has promised you the farm."

"But I'm not sure I want to be a farmer anymore. I have new skills now and could make a good living with them. But not here. There's no call for draughtsmen here in Johnstown or anywhere else in the county."

"What are you saying, Patrick? Where do you want us to live?"

Patrick shrugged and squeezed her hand before moving off again.

"Tonight's not the time for it. We can talk again."

Maura heard the impatience in his voice and felt the pit of her stomach turn to lead.

Two Days Later

Early morning and Maura trudged through the back pasture on her way to the well, the grass crunching under her feet, brittle with frost. She took a deep lungful of the cold air, happy to be outdoors after days of rain and howling wind. The well was situated close to a belt of trees, known locally as the fairy fort. Her mother had always claimed the sweetest water in the county came from their well, blessed as it was by the little folk. As she heaved the full bucket up on the rope, she hummed a tune her father had played on the tin whistle the night before. She glanced up and spotted Róisín approaching across the bottom field.

"Are you coming up to the house?" Maura called out to her. She waited for her to catch up.

"Aye, I need to talk to you." Róisín fell into step but Maura was on her guard. Róisín's words had an alarming ring.

"What's ailing you, Róisín? More trouble with Maguire? You know I can't intervene. He won't listen to the likes of me."

Róisín grabbed her arm. "Maura, my dear, I wish it was my trouble but — ."

Maura put the bucket down and turned to her. "If you've come making mischief for me and Patrick then I don't want to hear it."

"Don't be a fool!" Róisín exclaimed, tightening the grip on her arm. "'Tis bad enough he is playing you for one."

"Stop, Róisín! He would not do that."

Róisín pursed her lips, her blue eyes glowing with passion. "I've seen the proof myself, Maura. He's a cheat."

Maura shook her off. "Leave me alone!" She bent down and picked up the bucket, then stumbled away over the rough ground, her eyes blurred with tears.

"Maura, stop! You need to know the truth about him. He's come to an understanding with Kathleen Nugent from Ballymore," Róisín called out. "They met in New York and they came back on the same boat. The rumours are flying around her townland. Edward heard it all when he was up there at the mart yesterday."

Maura froze, all feeling in her body dropping to her toes. Slowly, she turned around. "I don't believe you. He would not do that to me. We're getting married in two weeks. It's all set."

"Have you seen him since he returned home?"

"Yes! Two nights ago."

"But not since? And was everything as it should be?"

"Well … I don't know for sure."

In two strides, Róisín caught up with her. "I hate being the one who has to tell you, sis, but I saw the pair of them last night. They walked past our house and on into Maguire's, brazen as anything, arm-in-arm. Edward says the Nugent's farm half the land out in Ballymore. She could have a dowry to rival anyone in the county and you know what Pat Senior thinks about money."

Maura shook her head. "He loves me. He told me so." The pathetic words seemed to hang in the air between them.

Róisín hugged her tightly and started to cry.

The following evening, Fr Murphy called to the house, his expression more stern than usual. Maura watched as her father bid him welcome and offered him a dram, as was his custom with any visitor. Her instincts screamed something was wrong. The priest barely greeted her and would not meet her eye.

Folding her sewing and putting it aside, she sat and waited, her heart heavy with sorrow and dread. All day she had thought about her sister's comments, struggling to find an excuse for Patrick's behaviour. But she knew Róisín would not lie about something so important. She hadn't told her father, fearing his temper would be roused.

The cleric took the glass of whisky. "Sláinte! And God bless ye all," he said before swallowing the lot in one go. Her father exchanged a surprised look with her. The glass was put down on the kitchen table. "I wish I were here on happier business, Eoin," the priest said. "But, I thought it best to come and see ye straight away with the news."

Her father waved him to a seat, looking perplexed.

"I had a visit from Pat Maguire Senior today."

"What has that to do with us?" Father asked, a sharp edge to his voice.

"Well, Eoin, 'tis best you sit down." The priest glanced across at her with such a sympathetic look, she had to grab the arm of the chair. "There is no easy way to say this. The reason he came to see me is that they want to call off the wedding. Patrick is returning to New York."

Her father swore and banged the table with his fist, making her and Fr Murphy jump.

There. It had been said. Róisín had been right. Maura fixed her gaze above the fire. Sound and light dimmed to nothing. Patrick was jilting her.

Half the village appeared anxious to console her. Sympathy and tea were administered but her humiliation burned and scorched. Their curious stares and the pregnant silences made her cringe. A lifetime of whispers would follow her now – there was no escaping that. Even those who came to the house declaring what a scandal it was and so close to the wedding too; they would talk about her and the family behind their backs for generations to come.

The first Sunday was the worst. As she entered the church, everyone fell silent. Her father's chin jutted out and he walked ahead of her down the aisle, proud as ever. He had to threaten her to make her accompany him. Even the wrath of the priest had seemed insignificant compared to the mortification of being a jilted woman in front of the congregation. Her face burned as she took her seat on the women's side of the church, sure all eyes were on her. Ahead, she could see Mrs Maguire and one of Patrick's sisters but there was no sign of him in the men's pews. As the whispers of the women around her rose, Róisín slipped in beside her and squeezed her hand. Maura bit her lip in an attempt to stem her tears.

Róisín proved to be her rock even if her bustling energy and straight-talking failed to soften the blow. However, she was practical. The wedding dress and veil disappeared from sight and with infinite patience she found out who had given which present and had Edward return the gifts to their family and friends. He came back with messages full of kindness at her plight. Maura could not bear to hear them; she wanted to curl up and die. She wasn't even sure what she was feeling. Grief? Anger? It seemed to be a mixture of emotions. It rankled that he hadn't even had the guts to tell her in person. And using Fr Murphy like that was despicable.

Her father didn't take it well. For a full day, he sat by the fire, staring into the grate, rigid with anger. He would speak to no one. On the second morning, he went out onto the land and stayed out all day. That evening he ate his dinner in silence and went straight to his bedroom. Maura listened in distress to the rumble of his prayers from behind the door. She envied him that release.

Then late one afternoon, Róisín came to visit, her face alight with news.

"Put that kettle on, Maura," Róisín said after hugging her and kissing their father on the cheek. "I have something to tell ye."

"Has that spalpeen changed his mind, then?" Father asked.

Róisín gave him an impatient look. "No! Even if he did, she'd be mad to have him back after the way he has treated her. He is nothing but a gutless —"

"I am here, you know," Maura said with a grimace as she filled the kettle.

Róisín's head swung around. "You need to pull yourself together. You've done nothing to be ashamed of. Where is your pride? Hold your head up and ignore the gossips."

"Easy for you to say! I'm the talk of Johnstown, if not the entire county. A little sympathy would be welcome."

"For goodness sake, Maura. It could have been far worse. You could have been with child."

"Róisín!" Father exclaimed. "None of that kind of talk!"

"Well, 'tis true, isn't it? She bears no shame."

Father shook his head. "Of course not, but —"

"What?" Maura cried, suddenly weary of it all.

"Nothing! I'm just sorry I didn't make him marry you before he left for America. That damned country gave him notions, it did."

Róisín gave an exasperated sigh and touched Maura's hand as she sat down. "When you hear this you'll have no excuse for moping. They are leaving in a couple of days. He and that Nugent girl are taking the boat back to America. They are to marry in New York at Christmas and good riddance, I say!"

Maura stared down into her cup. It would certainly be easier if he wasn't around to remind her of what might have been. But she was fooling herself; she would never forget him or stop loving him, despite what he was doing to her. When on her own, she tortured herself with questions because she didn't understand what she had done wrong; why this had happened to her. Now the future stretched out, fuzzy and unformed.

Father grabbed her hand and squeezed it hard. "He thinks little of his promises, the buck!" he growled.

Maura stirred the pot of stew absentmindedly. She knew her lethargy irritated Róisín. They had fought again and she hadn't visited at all that day or the day before. But how could her sister understand; it wasn't the love of *her* life about to disappear forever. With a sigh, she wondered where Patrick was and what he was doing, even though the very thought of him made her heart ache. Busy packing, no doubt. In her mind's eye, she could see his father lifting the heavy trunk onto the cart; much like the day she witnessed his first departure. He had kissed her goodbye in front of his family. She had been both embarrassed and proud. Would he spare a thought for her at all this time?

And that Kathleen Nugent. No doubt she was laughing at her and couldn't believe her good fortune in bagging a man like Patrick. *Her* Patrick. They had never met and she couldn't help wondering what she looked like, this woman who had stolen her man. Perhaps she was prettier, thinner or more intelligent? Not that it mattered if she had a large dowry to her name. Róisín was probably right. Pat Senior had done this, the greedy louse. Patrick had always done as his father told him. He'd probably been threatened into jilting her because Pat saw a fatter prize on the horizon.

Maura heard the door open behind her but continued her musings, staring down into the dark bubbling liquid in the pot.

"This won't be long, Father," she said.

No answer. She looked over her shoulder.

It was Patrick.

She caught her breath, unsure for a moment if she were dreaming. For a split second, she wondered if he had changed his mind and come back for her. But his demeanour wasn't promising.

"Hello, Maura," he said. He was twisting his cap in his hands, not quite meeting her eye.

She could only nod, not trusting herself to speak. Seeing him standing there when she had just been daydreaming about him was uncanny. But why had he come? Suddenly she was gripped by anger. He should have stayed away. Would anyone blame her if she flew at him and raked that handsome face with her nails? But she could not. To her astonishment, her anger fizzled out to be replaced by pity. That was unexpected and she almost laughed. Seeking composure, she rubbed her hands down her apron and watched his features closely. It was as if a huge chasm had opened up between them; a heart-rending distance full of dismay and regrets. She realised she had never really known him at all.

He gave her a pleading look. "Maura, I'm sorry, truly. I never intended to hurt you."

"Humiliate me, I think you mean," she said swallowing back her tears. "You have made me a laughing-stock."

"That was never my intention." He took a step towards her.

She held up her hand. "Don't! You knew exactly what would happen. They're all wondering what's wrong with me."

"No! Maura. Sure you're a grand girl, everyone knows."

"They're asking themselves why you've jilted me."

"People can be cruel."

"Yes, but I didn't expect it from you, Patrick. I thought you loved me."

To her amazement, he blushed an even deeper crimson. "I did, I swear and I know I deserve your scorn. I can only repeat how sorry I am at what's happened. I'm leaving. I … I thought it best to go back to America immediately, in the circumstances."

"That's awful kind of ye," she snapped. "I hope you and Miss Nugent have a pleasant journey." She wanted to scream her hurt at him like a banshee.

His face fell. "Oh! You've heard about that."

"You know this village. There isn't much happens without everyone hearing about it eventually."

"Maura, she's not a patch on you, believe me, but she has ambition. She loves America too and can see a life for herself there. You'd never want to leave Johnstown."

Maura stiffened. "You never asked if I wanted to go to America. You never gave me the opportunity to even think about it."

He shifted on his feet and looked down at the floor. "What's done is done."

From the shadow of the doorway, her father materialised behind Patrick. "Is that so?" he said. Maura didn't know how long he had been there or what he'd heard.

Patrick jumped and swung around before taking a few steps back, his face suddenly white. "Mr Hegarty!"

Her father nodded his head very slowly, staring at him hard, his face distorted by abhorrence. Then he glanced at her and his expression softened. "Are you all right, Maura? Has this spalpeen been bothering you?"

Maura shook her head. She didn't like the look on her father's face. She didn't like the fact that he had his hunting rifle in his hands. Strange, he hadn't said anything about going hunting today. The sack he used for his kills was hanging on the back of the door. Empty. Her heart began to pound.

"I've been looking for you, Mr Maguire," Father said, swinging his gaze back to Patrick. "I think you owe me an explanation."

Patrick looked at her nervously then back to her father. "I can understand that you are upset, sir, but I think it will be for the best. My future lies in America and Maura would never leave you … never leave here."

"Ah, I see you have convinced yourself you are doing the right thing by her by hightailing it back to America with some floozy in tow. Unfortunately, I don't quite see it that way. You see my problem is this. Before Maura's dear mother passed she made me promise to look after the girls, no matter what. So, I have little choice but to honour that promise even if you cannot be bothered to honour yours to my daughter."

"Father! Please stop this."

"No, my dear. I cannot let this blackguard treat you this way." Slowly, he raised the rifle, pointing it at Patrick's heart.

Patrick lunged at her and pulled her in front of him like a shield. A burning anger rose in Maura's throat as his fingers dug into her upper arms. Such a shockingly spineless thing for him to do. Patrick's breathing was thick and fast as it tickled the back of her neck. He was shaking with fear.

"Mr Hegarty — don't be foolish, what good can come of harming me? You'd swing for it!" Patrick said, stammering like a frightened schoolchild.

Her father cocked his head, a strange light in his eyes. His finger caressed the trigger.

Maura cried out. "Father, please. He's right! You'll hang if you kill him and then what will become of me?"

Her father frowned then slowly lowered the weapon. "Get out of my house, Maguire, and don't ever show your face on my land again. I detest rats. Next time I won't hesitate to shoot."

Patrick's hands slid away and he stepped around her. She could see the shine of perspiration on his forehead. Father gestured impatiently towards the door and Patrick almost tripped over his feet in his haste to escape. The door was left swinging behind him. Her father closed it with a snap before placing the rifle on the table. He began to laugh.

She turned on him, shaking with anger but also relief. "What's so funny? You shouldn't have threatened him like that! What if he goes to the police? What if you are arrested?"

"That excuse for a man? No, he won't do that. What's wrong with you, girl?" he asked, continuing to chuckle. "I wasn't really going to shoot him. Just wanted him to think I might." He sighed. "Though I admit I was sorely tempted. You've had a lucky escape. Now, don't just stand there gawping, I want my dinner."

The most difficult day was the one which should have been her wedding day. Maura could not bear to stay quietly at home. Once her chores were finished, she grabbed her coat and made her way to the village. Of late, she had formed the habit of visiting her mother's grave almost every day. Standing in the solitude and tranquility of the church grounds she could voice her anger, fears and regrets, albeit to a gravestone, without rebuke. Róisín and her father no longer wanted to talk about Patrick but she still needed to unburden herself.

As she neared the church, she saw a pony and trap approach from the far end of the village. It was Mrs Brookfield.

She pulled up along-side her. "Hello, Maura, I'm glad we've met. As it happens, I was on my way to see you. I wonder if we might have a wee chat?"

"I was just going in to visit my mother's grave," Maura said, torn between needing to find release for the turmoil in her heart, and being polite.

"Here is as good a place as any, I suppose, as there is no one around. I'll join you." She got down from the trap and tied the reins to the railing of the church.

Maura was both surprised and uncomfortable. Why didn't the lady wait outside for her? It was almost unheard of for a Protestant to enter Catholic church grounds. Whatever Mrs Brookfield wanted, it must be urgent. Her mind raced with possibilities but she couldn't fathom it out. They walked in silence along the gravel path which meandered through the grey Celtic crosses and lichen-covered headstones. At the rear of the graveyard, Maura stopped at the Hegarty plot and was relieved when Mrs Brookfield stepped back under the trees at a respectful distance. Quickly, she crossed herself and said a little prayer but she felt self-conscious knowing the lady was watching her. Far sooner than she would have liked, she crossed herself again and stepped back across the path.

Mrs Brookfield gave her a kindly smile. "Now, my dear, it is too cold to be standing around for long, so I will get to the point. I have a proposal for you. A friend up in Dublin has a haberdashery business and is looking for a young woman to help her out in the shop. You have an interest in sewing, I know, and I think you would be the ideal candidate."

Maura was taken aback. "But I have no training."

"There is no need to worry about that. She will train you up in no time. You are a good girl with plenty of common sense. She is very happy to take you on my recommendation."

This was so unexpected and absolutely terrifying. She had never left the county never mind going to a great big city like Dublin on her own. "Thank you, Mrs Brookfield, but I don't think so. I'd have to leave my father on his own —"

"But my dear, he has your sister and her husband to look after him. After what has happened to you, do you really think it is a good idea to stay here? It's time you spread your wings. After all, isn't that what Patrick Maguire has done?"

Maura couldn't deny the truth of that. A new beginning, away from Johnstown, was tantalising. If she stayed, she would always be the girl who was left at the altar; the girl who wasn't good enough for the Maguire's. And, worst of all, there would always be reminders of him everywhere she went.

"Can I at least tell her you will think about it?" Mrs Brookfield asked.

"I suppose so," she said. She looked about her; across the fields to the mountains in the distance and back over the village, the only place she had ever known. She would miss the place; miss her family, but only a life of drudgery awaited her here. "I will talk to my father. May I have a couple of days to think this over?"

Mrs Brookfield nodded and linked her arm as they made their way back to the road. "Don't wait too long, Maura. A chance like this doesn't come up very often."

Maura knew she was right but her curiosity was raging. "Forgive me, Mrs Brookfield, I don't wish to sound ungrateful, but why are you so eager to help me?"

Mrs Brookfield stopped just as they reached the gate. "Do you know about the suffragettes?"

"I've heard my sister talk of them."

"In my own way, I consider myself one ... well, at least in as far as it is possible living in rural Ireland. I too believe that women should have more control over their lives. Why must every young girl marry and bear children until she is wasted and old before her time? Why can she not have a career?"

"But it's how it has always been," Maura said. She had never given it much thought. Marriage had been the dream - a man and house of her own and all that entailed.

"That doesn't make it right. I'm not saying marriage is bad, but women should have other choices." Mrs Brookfield sighed. "This village is all you have ever known but trust me, there is a wonderful world out there waiting for you. Grab this chance and make the best of it." She gave her a long stare and Maura knew it would be difficult to resist her will. "I hope to hear from you soon. Good day to you, Maura," she said, untying the reins and hopping up into the trap with surprising agility for her age. "If your father is agreeable, let him come up to see me and we can sort out the details."

Maura watched her turn the trap and set off for home. Perhaps she was right. She would never be content here now. At least Dublin offered her a chance to emerge from the shadow of her family; of this tiny village with its small-minded attitudes.

As she set off for home, a funny thought struck her. Unwittingly, Patrick had done her an enormous favour. Instead of marital servitude, the promise of an independent life now beckoned. Dublin wasn't New York, but it began to glow like a beacon in her mind.

The End

The Gift

A Childhood Memoir

It was the summer of 1970. We were travelling cross-country to visit my mother's childhood home in Mayo, crammed into my father's wine-coloured mini, a ridiculous car for a man so tall. I wasn't sure about this trip. I missed my friends at home in Dublin already. Would they forget about me if I was gone too long? My mother sat in the front passenger seat. I recall her midnight-blue sleeveless top and the sunburnt patches on her shoulders where the skin was white and starting to peel. Her short light-brown hair curled and caught the sunlight, perfectly complimenting her freckled skin.

As we sped along, I was mesmerised by the unfamiliar landscape of neat, green fields, marked by trees, hedgerows and smart stone walls. So much space, so little concrete. To a Dublin Jackeen it was an alien world. Most of the fields we passed held cattle and I was proud to learn the breed from my mother. Friesians for the milk, she told me. Black and white, they stood, munching the grass with a slow rolling motion - much as I rolled the word Friesian around in my mouth, testing its novelty. What about the brown ones and the pure black ones? But she wasn't sure and so we resumed our game of *I Spy*.

The bog road had been mentioned several times in the days leading up to the trip and I was dying to see it. It's a great shortcut, my father said, cuts off half an hour at least. I was so impressed. How did he know about it? My childish brain tried to compute. Was it a secret passage? And what was a bog? We turned off the main road and I was plunged into a magical land. I was immediately struck by the empty brown-blackness and the tiny islands of green grass, quivering in the ruffles of breeze that sneaked along the cut banks. Reeks of drying turf dotted the terrain like prehistoric stones defying you to explain their history.

Pitted and scarred by centuries of turf cutting, the marshy land stretched towards the horizon in every direction. A sinuous, narrow road with grass growing in the middle, wound its way through, dipping and curving like a snake. Father drove fast over the hills so I would get the whooshing sensation in my stomach that he knew I loved. He smiled at me in the rear-view mirror.

Why were there no trees, I wondered. I wanted him to stop so I could get a proper look but my mother said you had to know what you were about in the bog. The bog holes were full of deadly peat water and the dreaded midges would eat you alive. You'd never be seen again, she said with a knowing glance at my father. I shivered, delighted.

All too soon, the bog was left behind and the landscape altered again. This was a wilder place, west of the Shannon. The poorest land in the country, my father said, good for nothing but grazing sheep. And now the land seemed sad to me with its irregular fields and wonky dry-stone walls. Sometimes rocks rose out of the ground, grey, jagged and lichen-covered. Trees carved by the wind held sway over this land, their branches like the crooked fingers of the old men I saw, standing about in every town we passed.

Now all that was to be seen were sheep, as my father had foretold. Why do they have coloured marks on their backs, I asked. They explained to me about branding. How clever, I thought, storing this little nugget away with all the rest. I was quickly becoming a country girl.

I remember suddenly feeling tired. We'd been in the car for hours it seemed to me. I kept asking how much longer and always received the same response — nearly there. My favourite teddy was my only companion in the back seat. Sometimes I held his paw because he looked a little frightened by all the newness. He needed reassurance. We passed a small house set up on a little hill, smoke climbing lazily into the sky from its chimney and I caught the first smell of burning turf — a smell that can still bring me back to the West in an instant. A woman in an apron stood in the garden and she waved and smiled as we swept past. I knew we were in Mayo now, for why else would she wave at us, and at my mother who was going home? What's her name, I asked, but my mother just smiled. Nearly there.

I will never forget my first view of the house. Square and white with black window-sills and a large front door with windows on either side. We pulled up in front, the gravel crunching under the tyres. Now my shyness kicked in. I was about to meet my aunt and uncle, and my cousins. My mother said I had met them before but I had no memory of it. My biggest fear was they would think I was stupid, not knowing anything about the countryside. Would they be impressed that I knew about Friesians? Grabbing my mother's hand tightly, we made our way up the path to the door. Teddy was safe under my arm.

"Well, hello there," my uncle said with a huge wide grin as the door swung open. "Ye made it, anyways."

We were ushered into the house. It was huge, much bigger than our semi-detached in Dublin. All that house, and only the four of them in it. Greetings made, we all sat down in the parlour. A huge red-brick fireplace dominated the room, the turf glowing orange in the grate, with two built-in seats on either side. I'd never seen anything like that before. I longed to sit on one of the seats but I was too shy to ask and remained on my father's lap, clutching Teddy tightly and listening to their talk.

It was a happy house and everyone smiled and bantered. My mother chatted and laughed, asking about this one and that, people I didn't know. This was homecoming and I enjoyed it vicariously through her. My cousins looked at me with curiosity and I snuck glances back. But my peace came to an end when my uncle asked was I always so quiet and was it because I was an only child? My mother gave me an impatient glance. I wanted to hide, guilt tearing at my calmness. My mother could never understand my shyness and I had no words to explain it to her. I hated being an only child and longed for the company of a brother or sister. Was it my fault? And why did adults always draw attention to my silence? It was my safe place where I could be invisible. But thankfully, the conversation moved on and I was relieved.

"You'll have a drop, won't you?" Uncle asked my father. He produced a glass bottle with a clear liquid inside. After pouring out, he handed round the measures to all the adults.

"Where did you get the poteen?" my mother asked with a grin, sniffing her glass before taking a sip. But my uncle just tipped the side of his nose and smiled.

The next day we were to *save the hay*, though I was not sure what kind of peril it was in. The long grass had been cut by the tractor the previous evening and now my uncle handed my mother and father the tools of the trade; hay forks. My cousin took me up the field. He was my new best friend, being just a few months younger than me. And he knew everything.

We watched the adults turning the grass over, so it would dry out. Slowly and methodically they moved up and down the field. I'm sure the sun shone and it certainly didn't rain, but perhaps it is the golden light of memory that colours it.

As the day progressed my shyness lifted enough to enjoy playing in the fields, skipping over ditches. When my cousin told me about the fairy-fort in the field next door, and how you'd be cursed and die if you harmed those trees, I was awestruck. The days that followed have now all merged together in my memory. But I know the grass was turned again and soon haystacks were built.

My cousin and I ran amok, weaving in and out of those grassy hills, breathing in the verdant summer smell. In the evenings, if the cattle had been moved, we played outside in the field beside the house. Other children appeared and soon there was a gang of us, chasing about the field trying to avoid the cow pats, nettles and thistles. And I belonged.

But if there was one blot on my happiness, it was the milk. My uncle brought me out to the shed one morning and I watched as he sat down on a three-legged stool beside a cow. I watched fascinated as the white liquid squirted into the bucket, foam forming on the top. But horror of horrors, the bucket was brought into the kitchen and some of the milk was poured into a jug on the table. The warm, creamy, frothy stuff was the only milk available. How I longed for the cold, pure white milk from the bottle! Needless to say, I was teased.

The hay no longer being in danger, we set out on a little excursion. When anyone asks me when I fell in love with Connemara, it dates from this trip. Dark brooding skies loomed above as we made our way south-west. I was disgruntled because I wanted to stay and play with my cousins and all my new friends. I may have sulked. But the sights that awaited me soon dispelled my mood.

There is magic and beauty, desolation and majesty in the hills of Connemara. Barren peaks and cold, dark lakes, twisting roads and vistas that shake the soul await you. The angry skies are often reflected in the black smooth surface of the water, with reeds standing proud as soldiers along the margins. Maybe it's a Celtic thing – this love of the melancholy, but it was so powerful I could not speak but pressed my nose to the window. The Twelve Bens. The name of those mountains stuck in my head and I'm thankful that my first sight of them was with my mother and father.

In the evenings there were the ghost stories. My uncle was very fond of them and every night, it seemed to me, he made sure I went to bed terrified. Tales of the banshee, omens of death and mysterious balls of light were recounted with chilling proficiency. I would follow my mother up the steep stairs to bed, my head full of his stories and my heart pounding like the devil. Compounding this, was the coal-black darkness of a country night, something I had not experienced before. After she tucked me in and said goodnight, I would lie rigid on my back, bedclothes tucked under my chin, my eyes fruitlessly searching the darkness for the dreaded unearthly visitor or ball of light; my ears cocked for a ghostly tread on the floorboards. My fascination for ghostly tales and the supernatural was most likely born on those nights.

But it was also a house full of music. My young cousins sang and played instruments, which impressed me greatly. My aunt sang *Danny Boy* one evening and almost had me in tears; it was so haunting and beautiful. My uncle had a band back in the day and was very fond of singing and playing the saxophone. Those memories are as rich and mellow today as when I first heard him sing about the sinking of the Titanic, *It Was Sad When That Great Ship Went Down*. If I close my eyes, I can still hear him sing it.

I'm sure I cried the day we left. I still recall the hollow feeling in my stomach as our car pulled away and I waved goodbye to my cousins, standing at the door. I desperately wanted to stay. It didn't help when my mother scolded me for my newly acquired Mayo accent. I, of course, was secretly quite proud of it.

We returned for other holidays over the following years but that first visit made the most impact on me. Only six years' later, my mother passed away and now, when I return to Mayo to the place she was born, I feel closest to her. She bequeathed a precious gift; an unshakable love of a place and its people.

The End

Mayday

Queenstown, County Cork, Friday, 7th May 1915
Valentine Lambert gazed at his reflection in the speckled mirror, aghast to see the effects of the previous night's celebrations so clearly marked, but it wasn't every day your only sister tied the knot. It had been two in the morning when he had finally collapsed into bed. Plunging his hands into the cold water, he braced himself for the shock as the liquid hit his face. He was fully awake now.

Pulling back the curtains, he grunted. A heavy fog obscured the usual view of Queenstown harbour with its bizarre jumble of fishing boats, naval vessels and ocean liners. The streets were always full of travellers, their faces alive with excitement or dread, depending on whether they were off on an adventure or escaping grinding poverty. He had often contemplated the trip to America himself and his small but growing savings account would someday facilitate it. But for now, he had to bear the monotony of working as a clerk for Perch Shipping Agents. Besides, the rumours of German U-boats out in the bay gave him and many others pause for thought. Several merchant ships had been targeted in the last few days. Even the fishermen were nervous.

As he walked down the hill towards the quay, he met his friend Joe, a fisherman on one of the larger trawlers.

"Are you grounded?" Valentine asked with a grin.

"No, this fog will burn off shortly, so we should get out before noon," Joe said. "You look like a ghost. Sore head?"

"You could say that! Have you recovered yourself?"

Joe chuckled and slapped his shoulder. "It was a grand night, wasn't it? Your Maggie looked fine."

"She did. They're heading off to Bantry to stay with his folks for a few days."

"Well for some!" Joe said, stifling a yawn before falling into step. "By any chance, have you thought about what I was saying last night?"

Valentine's heart sank; he had hoped he had forgotten and that it had been the drink talking. All of a sudden, Joe was mad keen to join the British Navy and wanted him to do the same. Queenstown was a naval base. Valentine reckoned Joe's head had been turned by the glamour of the uniforms, that and the fact the young women seemed to find them irresistible.

"It's not our fight, Joe."

"Nonsense! Our lads are being slaughtered too. Poor Michael Ryan last week."

"They chose to go and knew the danger," Valentine said smothering a twinge of uncertainty. Michael had been in school with them. "Our lives are here anyway until this damned war is over."

"Not everyone wants to go to America like you, Val," Joe said. "Besides, what future do I have on *The Agnes*? Da has already made it clear it will go to Frank. The best I can hope for is to work for my brother for the rest of my life. If I join the navy at least I'll see a bit of the world."

"But if you work for Frank your life would be your own. If you save hard, you'll have your own boat one day. Put that nonsense out of your head. Navy life is slavery and to a foreign power too."

Joe threw him an anguished glance as a couple of naval officers walked past.

Valentine shrugged and gave an impatient shake of his head before pulling out his watch. "I'll meet you later in Burke's for a quick pint, but I have to go now. Can't keep old Perch waiting; there will be hell to pay."

With a significant glance up at the clock, Mr Perch gave him a cool greeting, but the expected telling-off did not happen. Grateful to have escaped a tongue-lashing, Valentine slid behind his desk and opened the ledger. Was Perch going soft, he wondered. Valentine looked across at Martin his colleague who was busy scribbling away. He did not acknowledge him. With a sigh that touched off some fireworks in his hungover brain, he began to tot the long list of figures. The day was going to drag.

At lunchtime, he discovered the punishment for his tardiness; he had to take the late lunch slot. With a throbbing head and a dry mouth, he tried to concentrate on the letter he was drafting, but all he could think about was heading up to his favourite spot for his lunch and a quick nap. However, it was almost one-thirty when Martin appeared back in the office and he was free to go.

Despite the warmth of the day, Valentine shivered as he walked out the road. There was a strange haziness to his peripheral vision too, which he could only put down to the previous night's celebrations and lack of sleep. Or perhaps he was coming down with something.

On a fine day such as today, his lunchtime picnic spot was a welcome sight. Up on the hill, looking down upon the bay, you could see for miles. In the distance, past Spike Island, Roche's Point Lighthouse shone white on the headland and out beyond, the sea shimmered azure blue. Calm, beautiful and tempting.

Valentine hopped over the dry stone wall and sat down with his back to the warm stones. He took in the view and felt a pang of envy. His friend Joe was out on the boat and no doubt enjoying the afternoon sunshine. Wouldn't it be lovely to walk along the headland, with the likes of Annie Casey to keep him company? Knowing his luck, it would be raining tomorrow afternoon when he had his half-day. And no girl would walk out with him on a Sunday.

Lying down on the grass was a tempting idea but he knew

he was in danger of falling asleep. Perch would not be sympathetic if he were late again today. With a sigh, he unwrapped his sandwich from its brown paper. His stomach turned over; it looked even less appetising than usual. Perhaps he should move lodgings and escape Mrs Duffy's dire cooking? Leaning his head back against the wall, he pulled his cap down and closed his eyes. Just for a few minutes.

The water was deep and cold. Unseen hands were dragging him down into the darkness. Above him, macabre figures were flailing about in the water hindered by their clothes. He could make out suitcases, deckchairs and other things drifting around. Fighting towards the light he gasped for air as soon as he broke the surface. And all around him, people were moaning; the most dreadful of sounds. Soon the cold seeped into his muscles and made his limbs ache. Gradually, everyone stopped thrashing about. There was only the low moaning and the blank white faces of the dead suspended in the water.

He woke with a shudder, his mind humming with fear. After a few deep breaths the panic faded, but he was left feeling anxious. But it was the echo of one voice that disturbed him the most. Valentine shook his head as if to see more clearly; he didn't want her image to fade. The young woman had been quite beautiful, her pale face set off by a fine pair of green eyes and curls of chestnut hair. She was in trouble, this young woman, and she had pleaded with him for help. Ridiculous! He didn't even know who she was or where she was, or even if she was real. With trembling fingers, he pulled out his watch. Half-past two. Damn! He'd have to hurry back.

As he rounded the corner onto the quay, he noticed a huddle of people in the distance outside the Cunard office building. That was odd. He knew there was no liner due that day so it couldn't be the usual queue for tickets. Mystified, he continued along the quay towards his own office. Just as he pulled the handle, Perch tumbled out the door, closely followed by Martin, who was dragging on his coat. Both men looked flustered. Valentine grabbed Martin's sleeve as he passed. "What's going on?"

"Another U-boat attack!"

"What?"

A wave of dread washed over him. What if they were targeting fishing boats now? He knew every fisherman by name. He drank with them every other night. They were almost family.

"Have they torpedoed another merchant ship?"

Martin pointed towards the growing crowd further down the quay. "No! A liner - can you believe it? The mayday came in about half an hour ago."

"You can't be serious!"

Martin grimaced and hurried after Perch, leaving Valentine standing at the office door. His blood ran to ice as he recalled his dream.

The rumours spread through Queenstown with lightning speed. The Germans had torpedoed *The Lusitania* just off the Old Head of Kinsale. Someone said the ship was limping in with a gaping hole in her side. Someone else said everyone was lost and the ship had gone down. Valentine was torn between horror that the Germans would target a passenger liner and relief that his friends had not been the victims. And slowly the crowd outside the Cunard office grew.

Every vessel in the harbour prepared for launch but the British warships took two hours to get enough head of steam. Some of the smaller fishing boats were able to leave sooner but it was a two and a half-hour trip to where the stricken liner was said to have been hit.

Could anyone survive four hours in the cold water? Everyone prayed the fishing boats out of Kinsale would be there quickly enough to save lives. Valentine pleaded with a skipper and regardless of what Perch might say about it, he jumped aboard and headed out with the crew. He had to do *something*.

Huddled in the wheelhouse, the crew were silent for the entire journey. Valentine kept his eyes downcast, regretting the impulse to come out on the rescue trip. What use would he be to them? He didn't know what to expect; he'd only ever fished for mackerel for God's sake. Not bodies.

"Lord Almighty!" the skipper exclaimed.

Valentine heard the sharp intakes of breath of the men around him and slowly raised his eyes. The Old Head of Kinsale was to their right. But there was no sign of the huge ship. The water was thronged with people, bodies and debris. Some of the passengers wore lifejackets while others clung to pieces of wreckage. In the distance, Valentine could see a couple of overloaded lifeboats and some fishing boats doing their best to rescue people from the water. He recognised *The Agnes*, Joe's boat. It looked as though their decks were full. They were trying to get a towline to one of the lifeboats.

"Lads, get to it!" the skipper shouted.

For the next hour, they pulled shivering men, women and children from the water until they were in danger of being swamped themselves.

"Leave the dead," one crewman instructed him. Valentine wanted to object but he could understand why. He tried not to look at the lifeless bodies drifting in the water because he thought his heart might break. The worst was seeing the dead children, even infants, too small to survive the cold sea. They were beyond help.

"She went down so quickly. We didn't stand a chance," one man told him between sobs. "She listed so badly, they couldn't launch the lifeboats."

Valentine handed him the bottle of brandy, his throat tight with anger and despair.

Night had fallen by the time Valentine's boat tied up at the quay in Queenstown. A constant stream of miserable, cold survivors was helped off the boats. They seemed oblivious to their injuries, shock and horror etched on their faces as they walked along the harbour like automatons. The entire town had mobilised, and the sorry souls were whisked away to some of the hotels and guesthouses that lined the streets near the harbour. Dry clothes and food were offered by the townspeople.

The next boat was tied up and the crew began to carry off the dead. Valentine stepped up and offered to help. Fifteen bodies were brought up onto the quay in front of the Cunard office, each laid down on the ground. They didn't have enough sheets to cover them but they tried to lay them out with as much dignity as possible. More boats came in and soon the number of bodies had doubled, then trebled.

When there was no more room, two other temporary mortuaries were set up, one at Lynch's Quay and one up at The Arches. Some of the survivors walked down the line of bodies, desperately trying to find their loved ones. Valentine helped one man who was looking for his wife. He found the man's American accent difficult to understand but tried his best to comfort him. Perhaps she is up in the make-shift hospital or one of the guesthouses, he suggested. But they didn't find her on the quayside and the man was led away weeping.

It was then that Valentine spotted her; the young woman from his dream.

He wasn't even sure what made him look at the body so closely. His heart nearly ripped in two. Even in death, she looked serene. And very beautiful; with her hair spread out behind her head, dark and curling like seaweed. The only visible injury was a cut on her cheek.

"Do you know her, son?" A naval officer asked, touching his arm.

Valentine shook his head. The officer moved on but Valentine found he did not want to leave her. Could not leave her. Despair settled heavily in his heart. She had needed him, out there in the water, and he hadn't been able to help her. He didn't even know her name. Suddenly, he had a feverish need to find out what it was. Kneeling beside her, he put his hand into the pocket of her coat, desperate to find some means of identification. The cold soggy fabric clung to his hand and he shivered. The pocket was empty. He bent across and gingerly sought the other pocket with shaking fingers. With a gasp, he straightened up. He had felt a faint warm breath on his cheek as he leaned over her. As he scrutinised her face, he could have sworn he saw her eyelid move.

"Help!" he called out. "She's still alive!"

The End

Christmas at Malton Manor

Bristol, England, December 1884

It was almost Christmas. In a dreary drawing room in a wealthy suburb of Bristol, the twenty-four year old, auburn-haired and green-eyed Miss Kate Hamilton, sat staring at the meagre fire in the grate. She willed the feeling to return to her icy toes and the hands of the clock to move faster. Her pretty eyes were dull with boredom, a fact which would have astonished those who knew her well. But the position of companion to one of the dullest and meanest women in Britain had fallen to her lot. Frugality was good for the soul, Mrs Cartwright was often heard to proclaim. However, it was not an ideology she embraced when it came to her own portions at dinner, Kate had noted frequently.

Mrs Cartwright moved her great bulk, making her chair creak. "You know, Miss Hamilton, I have been thinking I would like to have my family around me at Christmas this year."

"I'm sure that would be most agreeable," Kate said, automatically.

"Yes, and of course it will involve a great deal of planning."

Kate was suddenly alert; she didn't like where this was heading.

"With my ill health, it cannot be expected that I would organise such an event. I will be relying heavily on you."

"But Mrs Cartwright, I will not be here, if you recall. I travel to Malton for my sister's wedding at the end of the week."

Mrs Cartwright's colour started to rise. "Well, you will

have to change your plans. You cannot possibly go if I need you here. Your loyalty is misplaced, I am sorry to say."

Not for the first time, the woman's capriciousness left her momentarily speechless. Goodness knows, the woman was not renowned for her generosity of spirit, but this was deliberately cruel.

"My sister will be so upset, Mrs Cartwright, for I am to be her bridesmaid," Kate said, hoping to penetrate the stone-like organ posing as a heart in her employer's enormous bosom.

"Poppycock! Anyone can be a bridesmaid. Your sister can hardly expect you to desert your employer for that. I am hurt, Miss Hamilton. I did not expect such ingratitude from you. Do you not realise how lucky you are to be employed in this house? My friends are forever telling me what a kind and generous employer I am." This was a favourite theme of Mrs Cartwright's and she went on for the best part of ten minutes exploring it.

Kate surrendered to defeat. This was an argument she could never win, but the prospect of spending Christmas away from home and missing the wedding was almost too much to bear. And all for the vanity of a woman who was universally disliked. Since her arrival in the house five months before, only one member of the lady's family had shown up and he had been a lecherous old goat who had tried to pin Kate up against the wall as they passed on the stairs.

Later that evening, as Kate made her way to her room at the top of the house, she succumbed to her pent-up fury. Muttering under her breath, she started to twist a lock of hair between thumb and index finger. Then froze. Whenever she did it at home, Mary would instantly look alarmed and beg to know what had angered her. With a pang of sorrow, she wished her wiser sister was here to consult. Fighting back her tears, she continued to her room.

When she had first arrived, she had such high hopes. Moving to Bristol was to be an adventure and a fresh start. It hadn't been an easy decision to leave Mary and the village where she had lived for most of her life. Demeaning, Mary had called her choice of new career. But entirely necessary, had been her quick response. Essential in fact, as Colonel Woodgate, who in her opinion did a disservice to the term local gentry, had closed the village school and she had lost her position. Without a reference she could not hope for another teaching post.

"He will do something for you, for I am sure he admires you greatly. If only you could bring yourself to apologise," Mary had said in the coaching yard of The Pelican the day she left. But she knew better. Two days before, some harsh words had been exchanged. The Colonel was a stubborn man. And she had her pride.

"Apologise! To that man? Never!" she had replied, picking up her suitcase.

"I will speak to him, if you wish," Mary said, swallowing hard, with tears welling up and threatening to fall.

"No, Mary, it is bad enough I have fallen foul of him." Valiantly holding back her own tears, she bid her sister farewell and boarded the coach for Bristol.

Now, months later, Kate's forbearance was frequently tested. Amongst Mrs Cartwright's many quirks was a great fondness for sherry. Frequently waking foul-tempered, she would take out her irritability on Kate and the servants. But Kate was trapped until such time she could inveigle a reference from her, so she had to tolerate the verbal assaults with a semblance of acceptance. To react was fatal. This she had learned in her first week, for Mrs Cartwright had a cruel streak and liked nothing better than to taunt and ridicule those under her thumb.

Unable to lash out, Kate focussed her ire and frustration on the man whose intransigence was the reason she was waiting hand and foot on a miserly widow, far from home. Even thinking of Colonel Robert Woodgate made her burn with anger. If he knew just how awful things were, he would probably think it hilarious. That was assuming he ever thought of her at all. She, on the other hand, would never forget their last encounter at Malton Manor. He had been in a rage, his black eyes flashing murder, the scar on his neck standing out white against the flush of anger. And to think she had felt sorry for him when he first arrived in the village – a wounded officer recently returned from the Transvaal. But it wasn't sympathy he needed in her opinion, it was locking up.

With a shake of her head, she tried to dispel his disturbing image from her mind. What was she to do? How could Mrs Cartwright be so nasty as to renege on her promise? She couldn't let her sister down and yet she could not afford to lose her position. Sitting down on the bed, she drew Mary's letter to her and read it once more. It overflowed with happiness, not least because she was expected home and they would have a few days together before Mary embarked on married life. Kate sighed. Pulling out paper and pen, she wrote the letter she knew would distress her sister. She had no choice.

A Few Days Later
After several sleepless nights, Kate had come to a decision. What had she been thinking? She would resign, for Mary was far more important than keeping her post. It was never going to end well anyway. Best to leave now, and with a bit of luck, she might be able to find another position after Christmas. But how to broach the subject with Mrs Cartwright? It held the promise of being an ugly confrontation. But she would have to do it today if she had any hope of making it to Malton on time for the wedding. She mulled it over as she walked slowly back towards Bleak House, as she liked to call it, having spent the morning running pointless errands for Mrs Cartwright. As she turned the corner, she saw a sleek black carriage standing at the kerb. Fearing it was the lecherous cousin returned, she slipped down the side of the house and made her way to the servants' entrance, only to find the kitchen was deserted. To her astonishment she found cook and Ruby the parlour maid

halfway down the hall, listening open-mouthed to the raised voices coming from the drawing room.

"Whatever are you doing?" Kate asked.

Ruby turned around. "Shush! There is such a to-do!"

"She'll skin you alive if she finds you out here eavesdropping," Kate said, skirting around them and making her escape up the stairs.

But she was no sooner in her room when Ruby came charging in. "You're wanted, Miss!"

"Does she not have a visitor? Couldn't you tell her I'm still out?"

"Sorry but she knows you're back."

"How?"

"I might have let it slip," Ruby replied, looking down at the floor.

"Oh, Ruby!" Kate exclaimed. The maid half-grimaced an apology. "Very well, I'll come directly. Who is the visitor?"

"No idea. Cook let him in. I was out back beating the rugs."

As Kate entered the drawing room, two pairs of eyes swung around; one pair grey and simmering with anger, the other as dark as molasses. She could not quite believe it, for the two people in the world she most disliked were facing each other across the room. The atmosphere positively fizzled with tension. She was instantly on her guard.

"Well, madam, what have you to say for yourself?" Mrs Cartwright said, taking a step towards her.

"Nothing at all," she said, "for I have no idea what is going on." She looked between the two.

"Don't you now! Somehow I doubt that. I guessed you were a little schemer the minute I saw you and now I have the proof." Mrs Cartwright pointed at Colonel Woodgate. The gentleman was looking his usual grim self, dressed in unrelieved black and filling the room with quiet menace. Striking features, broad shoulders and military bearing made him difficult to ignore and if she hadn't seen his darker side, she might even have been impressed by him. She knew he did not suffer fools and for a moment she enjoyed the knowledge he must be finding her employer an absolute horror. But he quirked a brow and if she wasn't mistaken, there was mischief lurking behind his dark gaze. She knew immediately he was enjoying himself. And most likely at her expense.

"Would Colonel Woodgate care to explain why he is here?" Kate said, staring at him pointedly.

"He says," Mrs Cartwright jumped in before he had a chance, "he is here to take you home."

Woodgate shrugged, all innocence, but she spotted his bottom lip twitch.

She deliberately turned away from him. "I know nothing of this," she said to Mrs Cartwright. This was just typical of Woodgate – interfering in what was none of his concern. "I did not ask him to come."

"You cannot mean to miss your sister's wedding, Miss Hamilton," he said at last, his tone sending an icy chill down her spine. She smarted at his accusation and threw him an angry glance. As if she would deliberately hurt her sister if she could avoid it. Did the stupid man not realise she was compromised?

"Her services are required here," Mrs Cartwright said, glaring at him. "I have not given my permission for her to leave." She turned to Kate. "I don't pay you to gallivant about the country and certainly not for such a frivolous reason as a wedding." Kate smarted. She doubted Mrs Cartwright had ever indulged in anything frivolous in her entire life.

"It would appear you must choose between us," Woodgate said, picking up his hat and gloves from a side table. Clearly, he was eager to leave and a tiny flicker of panic ignited within her. Much to her surprise, she wanted to go with him.

"I warn you, missy, if you abandon your post and leave with this person, you will not return to this house. I will not have my good nature impinged upon," Mrs Cartwright said with all her chins wobbling in unison. With a sniff she sat down and stared straight ahead, her face set.

A coiled snake of anger slowly began to unfurl. Kate breathed out slowly as it was the only way she could control the urge to let fly. Mrs Cartwright looked very sure of herself and Woodgate was regarding her with a quizzical expression, tapping his gloves against his leg. Feeling humiliated, she wanted to tell both of them to go to blazes. Either way, her time in this house had come to an end, thanks to the colonel; little did he realise he had saved her the trouble of doing it herself.

The journey would be loathsome, but it gave her comfort to know he would find it equally unpleasant.

"So be it! I'll be ready in five minutes," she said to him. He nodded and she thought she saw a flicker of approval. As she fled the room, she heard a gasp of rage from her soon-to-be ex-employer.

From the top of the stairs she could see Woodgate was waiting down in the hallway, peering out the window. He was leaning heavily on his cane, and she wondered if he were in pain. She had always been curious about his injuries, though he never referred to them. The scar on his neck was the only visible evidence, but she knew from David Alexander, her sister's fiancé and Woodgate's closest friend, he had taken a bullet in the leg at Majuba Hill. How fearsome he must have looked in uniform, for he was intimidating enough in civilian clothes.

Perhaps it was a trick of the light, but he looked more gaunt since she had seen him last. The planes of his face were stretched sharply across his high cheekbones and the silvery threads at his temples, which she had thought distinguished when first they had met, appeared more abundant. As she began to descend the stairs, his gaze turned upon her, leaving her suddenly self-conscious as she struggled with the weight of her suitcase, carpet bag and umbrella.

Ruby appeared just as she reached the bottom of the stairs. "Are you really going, Miss?"

"Yes, I must. You know it was only a matter of time and I am needed at home."

Woodgate frowned and came forward looking impatient. Ruby flicked him a nervous glance and stepped aside.

"I am glad to hear your sense of duty has returned, Miss Hamilton. Let me take that," he said, looking at her suitcase. Pride made her shake her head, but his fingers closed around her wrist, exerting gentle pressure. She released the handle, but held his gaze as defiantly as she dared.

"Say your goodbyes quickly. I want to reach Malton Manor before dark." Without a backward glance, he opened the front door and strode down the path.

Ruby stole a glance at the drawing room door. "Lord, we're for it now! She'll be impossible for days."

"I'm sorry, Ruby, but I can't stand it here any longer."

"There's not many can! Don't you worry about us, Miss. I'm only sad cos I lost my bet with cook, see. She said you wouldn't last till Christmas. I reckoned Easter."

Kate smiled. "I have let you down then. I'm sorry."

"Not to worry, I might get lucky with the next one. The old cat won't last long without someone to boss around. Some poor unfortunate will take your place within the week."

"Ruby, why do you put up with it? Why don't you look for another position?"

The maid jerked her head towards the drawing room door.

"She won't give me a reference. I'm stuck and she knows it."

There was no likelihood she would receive a reference either. She had wasted five months in needless servitude. But there was no point in crying over it now.

"Take care, Ruby," she said as she stepped outside.

"I will, Miss. Goodbye," Ruby said. The door closed behind her with a bang.

Kate took one last look up at the imposing facade, relieved she would never have to return. All she had to do was get through the next few hours and she would be back in Bramble Cottage. But when she turned to face her nemesis, she discovered he was waiting at the door of the carriage, looking rather grumpy. Piqued, she walked down the path as slowly as she dared.

"Good of you to join me, Miss Hamilton," he said, as she took his hand and entered the carriage. Once he was settled on the seat opposite, he rapped the roof with his cane and the carriage pulled away. His face set, he stared out the window, ignoring her completely.

She bit back a retort, her instincts telling her he was in a peculiar mood. Obviously, he hadn't come in the guise of a knight in shining armour for he disliked her far too much. But it begged the question, why had he come? She regarded him surreptitiously. So far his manner was brusque to the point of rudeness. Had Mrs Cartwright irritated him that much? If it had been anyone else subjected to the woman's stupidity she would have felt sorry for them, but it served him right for poking his long nose into her business.

"Colonel, as much as I appreciate being escorted home, I don't quite understand why you came for me," she said after several minutes of silence. "You could have saved yourself the trouble, for I intended to resign today."

Turning away from his contemplation of the passing streets, he glowered at her. "Indeed! Leaving it rather late, though, were you not?"

Kate felt a blush rise in her face. "Clearly, you do not understand the position I found myself in."

"Correct! I cannot think of any possible reason other than a wilful disregard for your sister's feelings. David and I were with her when she received your extraordinary letter. Frankly, I was shocked you could do such a thing. She was inconsolable. As I had business in Bristol, I volunteered to try my powers of persuasion."

"On Mrs Cartwright? I'd like to have witnessed that. She is the most intransigent woman alive."

"On you, Miss Hamilton. Your sister was counting on you being her bridesmaid."

"I would never do anything to hurt her. I was trying to avoid returning as a dependent on a newly-married couple. I do not believe David would thank me for it. It may take me months to find another position."

"I doubt he would see it in that light. David already regards you as a sister and holds you in high esteem. You have far too much pride for your own good, Miss Hamilton."

"It wasn't a decision I took lightly," she said through clenched teeth. "Mary understands the situation. I was lucky to secure that post and could not risk losing it. But on reflection I knew I would not be able to live with myself if I let Mary down."

"Why could you not have saved your sister all that heartache by handing in your notice and coming home as soon as that witch rescinded her permission? We could have avoided all of this high drama."

"References!"

"I beg your pardon?"

"I have no references. By quitting I would have been unlikely to receive one from her and you can be sure one won't be forthcoming now. She's far too mean-spirited. When the school closed, Reverend Atkins also refused to furnish me with one."

"Only because you called him … what was it again?"

"That's irrelevant," she said hurriedly, highly embarrassed at the memory.

"Hardly, Miss Hamilton. Your behaviour has become increasingly irrational of late. Besides, if you were a trifle more humble you would realise there are any number of people who would be willing to help you find employment, me included."

Kate sniffed in derision. "Is that so? Have you a vacancy

for a scullery maid at Malton Manor, perhaps?"

His eyes lit up. "I doubt you are sufficiently qualified."

She gave him a withering look. "Why would I accept help from you? By turning up today you forced the issue and made my position untenable … yet again."

"But you just said you were going to resign, anyway. And what do you mean *again*?"

"Oh come, please don't play innocent with me, Colonel. Malton School? If I didn't know better, you are deliberately trying to sabotage –"

"Be careful! I'm not in the mood for absurdity. What possible reason could I have to do you harm?" he asked, leaning towards her, his brows drawn together. She could almost feel his breath on her cheek, he was so close. A tantalising scent crept into her consciousness. Sandalwood – warm, dark and intriguing.

She sank back against the seat, suddenly shocked at the direction of her thoughts and the strange sensation coursing through her. "I ask myself that question quite often."

He sat back and shook his head. "Ridiculous! Your misfortune has been of your own making. There was no need for you to run away to Bristol in high dudgeon."

"I did not run away, Colonel!"

That damned eyebrow rose in mockery. "Hanbury School would have made a position available to you in due course. The case to merge the schools was sound, both financially and educationally. The building in Malton was not fit for purpose. How many times did you complain to us about it?"

"And you and the other governors would not listen. A little investment and it would have been viable. The school was the heart of the village. We will never attract young families to Malton without it."

"A school is no use if there is no work locally for the parents. Only five pupils. It was unsustainable. You must see that." He gave an exasperated sigh. "I don't want to argue with you about it. It is over and done."

Kate took a deep breath. There was no reasoning with him. He could never feel the same way about the village or Malton Manor, which was now his home, but had been her family home many years before. Despondent, she determined not to engage with him and turned her gaze out the window. Soon the city was left behind and the barren winter landscape of skeletal trees and empty fields reflected her mood perfectly.

Robert leaned his head back against the squabs and watched Kate turn away. A knot of concern was growing in his stomach. Overriding his relief at having extracted her from the control of that unspeakable woman was concern for her welfare. In the time he had known her, he had never seen her so subdued. Where was the infuriating, impetuous and lovely termagant gone? She had lost weight, too, which he guessed was down to the charming Mrs Cartwright's miserly housekeeping and general tyranny.

When he had learned she would not be coming back as planned, he had almost panicked. He had counted on it being an opportunity to talk her into coming back permanently. Luckily, some quick thinking and a small white lie about business in Bristol meant he had been able to come to the rescue, as pathetic as that sounded even to his own ears. Mary had been profuse in her thanks and only David seemed to suspect there might be an ulterior motive.

He hadn't quite expected Kate to fall on him in gratitude, but her hostility was a surprise. Their relationship had been tempestuous at times, but he had always thought there was an underlying respect, perhaps more. He had only realised the depth of his own feelings when she left so unexpectedly. The intervening months had been torture, his only source of information being David and the occasional reference by Mary. Worst of all, he felt incredibly foolish at the age of thirty-two to be so consumed by self-doubt.

But Africa had changed him; had changed everything. He had been lucky to escape with his life, but what did the future hold? His plans lay in tatters. Alice, his fiancé, had broken off their engagement. Angry and hurt, he had bought Malton Manor unseen just to get away from his family and, most of all, the pity. Alice's remarks had cut him to the bone; she had made it clear no woman would want to look upon his injuries. Indeed, he flinched whenever he caught a glimpse of his wounds reflected in a mirror or window. And the beautiful Kate – was he just a cantankerous cripple to her? But on those brief occasions when they had managed to find accord, he had felt relaxed and content in her company. And when those green eyes lit up with mischief, he wanted to lose himself in those emerald depths …

He shifted in his seat, trying to find a more comfortable position. Travelling by coach on long journeys was something he tried to avoid as the confined conditions always made his injured leg hurt abominably. But he had no choice as there was no rail link between Malton and Bristol. His leg was starting to throb now. Slowly, he eased it into a straighter position only for a cramp to strike, causing him to suck in a sharp breath.

Kate's head swung around, her eyes wide. "What's the matter?" she asked.

All he could manage was a shake of his head as the excruciating pain shot down the back of his leg. Gripping the edge of the seat, he pushed the pain-wracked leg hard against the opposite seat. The intense pain gradually began to ease.

Kate clutched his arm. "Colonel? Are you in pain?"

He exhaled slowly. "Don't fuss! I'm fine."

"Clearly, you are not!" She appeared to be truly concerned, her eyes full of pity.

It was the last thing he wanted to see.

"Has it been bothering you all day? Is that why you are in such a crotchety mood?"

He glared at her. "I'm not in a mood!"

She released his arm, much to his disappointment. He kneaded the tight muscle where the bullet had torn into it and as the spasm eased, he straightened up again.

"We cannot continue if you are unwell."

"It is only cramp and almost gone," he said, wanting to make light of it.

She didn't look convinced. "It's the long journey, isn't it?"

He nodded. "You should not have come all this way, if this is how travelling affects you."

"Someone had to put a stop to your foolishness."

Her eyes flashed daggers. "Have I ever told you how utterly charming you are?"

"I believe I am famous for it!" he said with a grimace.

Kate shook her head, then glanced down at his leg. "Why do you never speak of your time in Africa? What happened to you there?"

"It's not a subject I wish to discuss with a lady," he said, all of a sudden feeling defensive.

"I read the newspapers at the time. I'm not completely ignorant of the facts."

"Then you already know more than enough."

She tilted her head. "I may nag you until you do tell me, and it is going to be a *very* long journey, I promise you."

Could he risk opening up to her, to any woman for that matter? Desperately, he tried to think of a way to deflect her. "That unholy creature Cartwright has been a bad influence on you."

Two dimples appeared. "It is such a shame you didn't meet her under different circumstances, for I do believe she is looking for another husband, or perhaps I should say victim. Cook maintains she poisoned the late Mr Cartwright."

"I'd say it was a happy release for him in any event."

"I can't argue with that," she said with a tiny smile which encouraged her dimples to appear again.

How in God's name was he supposed to resist her? But he found clenching his hands helped relieve the urge to kiss her senseless.

He cleared his throat.

"Had you left your wits at home the day you agreed to become her drudge?"

"I was not her drudge; I was her *companion*."

He sniffed. "That would imply a level of respect which I did not discern."

Kate glanced away, her hands tightly clasped in her lap. "She was the only employer in Bristol who would accept someone without a reference. At the time I was grateful and relieved to find a position, but I see now it was deliberate on her part. Much as I hate to admit it, you are right. She wanted a slave, not a companion. And don't you dare say it was the comeuppance I deserved," she said, throwing him a nasty look.

"I do not need to," he said, "for you have just done so."

Kate woke the following morning to the smell of freshly baked bread. It felt wonderful to be back in her old bedroom under the eaves of Bramble Cottage. After a luxurious stretch, she bounded out of bed, grabbed her dressing gown and flew down the stairs to the tiny kitchen.

Mary grinned at her. "Morning, lazybones! Sit down, I've poached some eggs."

"Lovely! My, you have been busy. Have you been practising your housewifely skills?"

"Don't be impertinent!" Mary handed her a plate, piled with food and grinned back at her. "How did you sleep?"

Kate cut a slice of bread. "Very well. There is nothing like your own bed. I hadn't realised how much I missed this old place. I cannot wait to explore the garden."

"You missed your roses?" Mary asked.

"Yes and being able to sit under the old crab apple tree on a hot summer's day."

"I knew you must be homesick. I said it to David only last week. Your letters had become increasingly dull, my dear, and I did wonder if things were difficult in Bristol."

Kate had confessed everything to her the night before as

they had chatted over the fire until the early hours of the morning.

Kate grimaced and put down the bread knife. "It was a terrible mistake and I wish I had left her sooner. Then perhaps I would have my dignity intact."

"What do you mean?"

"The colonel – it was humiliating. He even dared to lecture me on familial duty!" she said, rolling her eyes.

"Ah!"

"What does that mean?"

"My dear sister, are you blind? The poor man is besotted."

Kate started to laugh. "Please! Don't be ridiculous. He dislikes me and never misses an opportunity to –"

"David is convinced of it," Mary cut in, pursing her lips before picking up the teapot and starting to pour.

This was startling, but surely someone as private as Woodgate would not even hint at such a thing. Besides, he had made it plain he thought her impulsive, irrational and silly. "Has Woodgate actually said something to him or is David just as delusional as you?"

"But you are curious all the same." Mary smiled one of her cheeky smiles. "I know you are."

Kate was burning with curiosity – who wouldn't be on hearing something so fantastical? But she would not admit it to Mary, for she knew she would be teased relentlessly. However, a strange and uncomfortable sensation was growing within her and for some reason, his dark intense gaze popped into her head. "It is nonsense. The man barely tolerates me."

"It's what he doesn't say, Kate, that is significant. Look at the facts." Mary started to tick off her fingers. "In all the years he has been living at Malton Manor do you ever recall him going to Bristol or even mentioning it?"

"No."

"It was an excuse to fetch you, I'm convinced of it."

Kate laughed and shook her head.

"And, it is well known he avoids long journeys because of his injuries. Why would he put himself through that if not driven by some very strong feelings?"

Kate shrugged and buttered her bread, hoping she'd stop.

"And most significant of all, despite the local belles and their mamas in open pursuit, he has withstood all and remains unattached," Mary said, looking pleased with her arguments.

"You speak of his feelings – I have only ever noticed the nasty variety. You are reading far too much into his actions. No doubt he saw it as an opportunity to act superior and be ghastly, and he was. He is still smarting over the school debacle and wanted to humiliate me."

"No. It is you who can't let that go. It has worked out well, if you are interested."

"But it is such a distance for the children to travel when there is a perfectly fine school building in the village," she said.

"For heaven's sake, Kate! The colonel hired Peter Morris to bring them back and forth to school in his gig every day. What do you say to that?"

Kate looked up, astonished. How thoughtful and kind; she had underestimated him. "I am glad to hear they do not have to walk that distance, particularly in the winter."

Mary suddenly grinned. "So you see, the colonel isn't as black as you want to make out. But I see you are not convinced."

"Correct!" Kate said, popping the last of her bread into her mouth.

"Then explain to me why my wedding is to take place in the chapel at Malton Abbey and the colonel is hosting our wedding reception in the Manor. It is all arranged."

Kate stared at her sister. "Your wedding is at the abbey, not St Mark's?"

"Yes, isn't it wonderful?"

"How extraordinary! Why would he do that? He never entertains there."

"Exactly! He told David he was offering it because it was our family home at one time and if our parents were still alive, it is where the ceremony would have been held."

"You see! He has done it for you," Kate said, nursing a sudden twinge of disappointment.

"You believe what you wish, Kate. Of course I'm delighted, but I don't think it is for my benefit at all. Now eat up, for we have lots to do and only two days to go."

The days that followed were so busy that Kate had barely a minute to think about the colonel or her sister's assertions. David was a constant visitor and in exasperation, Mary told Kate to take him out from under her feet, so she coaxed him out for a walk. She was glad to have the opportunity to thank him for making Mary so happy and for all he had done for them.

"You do know you are welcome to come live with us? I know Hanbury doesn't hold the same draw for you ladies as Malton, but it does have its merits," he said, as soon as they had left the outskirts of the village.

"Of course and thank you, but it will not be necessary. I will find another position shortly."

"You are independently minded, Kate, and I admire you for it, but if you ever change your mind, know that you would be welcome. At the very least, I will expect you to spend Christmas with us, every year," he said. She nodded, unable to speak as she found there was a lump in her throat. They strode on down the narrow road in companionable silence. The air was crisp and the hard frost of the night before still lay in the shadows. Kate felt at peace, back in familiar surroundings. This was one of her favourite walks, with ancient oaks lining the road and the sound of the river gurgling over the rocks in the valley below. She had promised herself she would not think about her situation until after the wedding and fully intended to enjoy her time back in Malton.

Soon the sound of horses could be heard approaching at

great speed. Around the corner came a large and well-appointed travelling carriage. Kate and David jumped up on to the grassy bank as it passed. An elderly white-haired lady was inside and, as it drew alongside, she acknowledged them with a queenly nod.

"That's Mrs Woodgate," David said, as they watched the carriage speed away.

"The colonel's mother?"

"Yes, he said she was coming to stay for Christmas. I don't think he was pleased about it as she gave him very little notice, but with the wedding in the house, I'm sure he will be glad of her help."

"I can see a resemblance."

"Yes, it is quite marked, but their manner is different. Mrs Woodgate is charm itself."

"Has she been here before? I do not recall any of his family paying visits."

"No, this is her first time. I met her in Kent when I accompanied Robert there last summer."

"Is his father still alive? I don't believe I've ever heard him mentioned."

"Yes, he is, but bedridden, I'm afraid, so I didn't see much of him at all."

"But is it not odd that his mother has not visited before? Was there a falling-out?"

David smiled, looking down at her with a knowing look. "I think we both know that is quite possible. Robert doesn't hold fire as much as he should." He stopped suddenly. "You know, what he really needs is a softer influence, someone to take away that black cloud that hangs over him sometimes. Someone like –"

"Stop! I am getting enough of that nonsense from Mary."

David chuckled and patted her arm. "From tomorrow I will be your brother, Kate. You send him to me if he comes up to scratch. I'd like nothing better than to have the upper hand for once. It would be entertaining to make him think I would withhold my consent." David suddenly blanched. "Perhaps it wouldn't be such a great joke. He might run me through."

Kate shook her head in exasperation. "Well, I'm sorry to disappoint you, David, but I do not believe the occasion will arise."

"We will see," he said, sounding very smug.

Mary & David's Wedding Day, 23rd December

At the appointed time, the Malton Manor carriage arrived to pick up Kate and her sister. Once seated, they held hands for the short journey, each deep in thought. Kate's stomach was churning with nerves. The notion that the colonel was partial to her had taken hold and she had lain awake the night before trying to figure out what her own feelings were. Dawn had arrived and she was none the wiser. Yes, he was attractive and the thought of spending the rest of her life with him wasn't exactly repugnant, but his actions and words did not proclaim the lover at all. And although it was tempting to dream of the rose garden at the Manor, would it be worth it to live with someone so cold and forbidding?

"I'm so glad you're here, Kate," Mary said, squeezing her hand and breaking into her thoughts. "I don't think I could have faced this alone."

"I was an idiot, Mary. I should not have let you think I had abandoned you. Can you forgive me?"

Mary kissed her cheek. "Of course, my dear."

The carriage pulled into the long carriageway that led up to the house. Kate had mixed emotions as she surveyed its sandstone facade and red high-pitched roof. The park was extensive with both woodland and formal gardens. To the side of the house was the walled garden where she had learned about roses with her mother. And on the far side were the remains of Malton Abbey, with only the chapel still in use, the walls of the cloisters in ruins. They had played there as children.

As the carriage pulled up outside the chapel, Kate spotted

a portly gentleman in full morning dress, rubbing his hands and stamping his feet. It was Uncle Matthew. Thankfully, David and the colonel, who was acting as his best man, were already inside.

"It was good of him to come all this way to give me away. I didn't dare hope when I wrote to him," Mary said. "It is such a shame Aunt Helen is too ill to travel."

The door opened and the steps were let down. "Goodness me!" Uncle Matthew said. "Such fine ladies!" Each was embraced in turn.

Kate handed Mary her bouquet. She had made it for her, using holly and ivy from the garden at Bramble Cottage. She had even found a couple of roses in a sheltered spot and by peeling away their damaged outer petals found they were good enough to use. Mary stood biting her lip, looking every inch the nervous bride.

"You look wonderful," Kate said. And she did. Her blue eyes were brimming with laughter and excitement. The white lace gown was perfect and with her dark blonde hair dressed high on her head and her cheeks glowing, she looked almost regal.

Mary tilted her head and looked her up and down. "I'm so glad I choose those colours for you. They bring out your colouring to perfection."

Kate looked down at her pale green and cream silk dress. It had been a wonderful surprise from Mary that morning. She had never owned anything so pretty. "Thank you, I love it more than I can say."

"Ladies, it is rather chilly. Shall we?" Uncle Matthew said, proffering his arm to Mary. "I do believe there is an anxious young man waiting for you inside."

The chapel had been restored by Kate's great-grandfather. She had forgotten how beautiful it was, its Catholic origins obvious in its highly decorated walls and beautiful vaulted ceiling. Recollections of her childhood came swooping back:

sitting holding her mother's hand during Sunday service; being scolded for fidgeting in church and listening to her father's rich baritone echo around the walls as he read the lessons. The emotion of the day was bringing back some long-buried memories. Sitting beside Uncle Matthew, she swallowed hard. She hadn't realised how difficult it would be to come back to her old home. She tucked her arm through Uncle Matthew's. He must have been in tune with her thoughts, for he smiled back with a look full of sympathy.

She tried to concentrate on the ceremony. But as her gaze swept across the chapel it fell on the colonel, sitting so still and yet managing to exude an aura of coiled energy. She felt heat rise in her face. Good God, she wasn't going to turn into one of those silly females who lose their wits over a handsome face? This was lowering indeed. Could she survive the entire day without saying or doing something foolish? But she had to admit he looked well in full morning dress and she had never noticed the way his hair curled very slightly just above the stiff white collar. If only Mary and David hadn't put such silly notions in her head about him. It was preposterous, of course, but there was something a little flattering about it, too.

Suddenly dismayed at where her thoughts were leading, she looked back at the Reverend Atkins. There was a sight to kill all romantic thoughts in a young lady's head. Small in stature, bald, and stout, he had on first coming to the parish indicated an interest in her. Her rebuttal had several unfortunate consequences, not least his backing of the school closure. She suspected he had run to the colonel with tales about her on many occasions, but could never prove it. Even today his gaze, when it did rest on her, was cool to the point of icy. Kate ducked her head, suddenly wanting to giggle. If she wasn't careful she would become known as a difficult and highly strung troublemaking spinster. Only the night before, Mary had pleaded with her to avoid any confrontations, at least until she and David had left after the reception.

Soon the service was over. How was it possible to be

happy and sad at the same time? Her little family was broken up now forever. No more sitting over the fire putting the world to rights; no more lazy summer afternoons out in the garden, sitting under the trees, lulled to sleep by the drone of insects.

But to see Mary so happy was a joy. If she had to lose her sister to anyone, she could not have chosen better than David. It was easy to see he adored Mary. He had beamed throughout the entire ceremony, through the signing of the register and the walk down the aisle. While the obligatory photograph was being taken, he clutched Mary's hand as if he would never let go.

It appeared the entire village of Malton had come to see the happy couple and wish them well. A cheer went up when Mary and David stopped at the chapel door and there was a great deal of laughter as David stood on the chapel steps and threw coins up in the air for the village children to scavenge. Kate stood behind with the colonel, having followed the bridal couple down the aisle with him.

"I don't like the look of that sky, Miss Hamilton. We should make our way to the house," he said.

Kate followed his gaze towards the west. The sky was leaden grey and the wind had dropped. She shivered.

He looked down at her. "You must be cold. A coat might have been a good idea. It is winter, after all."

"But, Colonel, you know well I am never sensible. But I will put your mind at rest: I left it in the carriage."

"I doubt ..." he paused and seemed to be struggling for words. "Never mind! Come, if we lead, the others will follow."

A lavish breakfast had been laid on in the dining room of Malton Manor and the thirty or so guests were entertained by a string quartet. The house had been decorated for the season, with a beautiful Christmas tree standing proud in the hallway.

"This is all so grand," Mary whispered in Kate's ear. "I

wonder who he is trying to impress?" Kate gave her a warning glance, but Mary beamed back at her. "Now we must leave, Kate, if we are to make it to Hanbury before the weather closes in." She kissed her cheek. "Take care and I will see you in a couple of days."

The bridal couple were given a rousing send-off from the front steps. Once their carriage was out of sight, Kate linked her uncle's arm as they turned to go back inside.

"You will miss her, my dear. Perhaps you should come back to Bath with me," he said. "I don't like the thought of you here on your own."

"You are very kind, but I will be fine for a couple of days. I'm far from helpless," she said, smiling at him.

"We have many connections, my dear. If you are determined to find a position, why not let us help you? Your aunt and I would love to have you near us in Bath."

"That is generous of you, Uncle. I will certainly think about it."

"Excellent," he said.

"Do you intend to return to Bath this evening? I am sure you are reluctant to leave Aunt Helen alone for long."

"I am happy to say that she is on the mend, my dear, and she was most particular in sending her regards to you. You know how she worries. She won't be happy until she sees you wed, too."

Kate gave him a knowing look. Her aunt's letters invariably touched on the subject. "You may tell her it is unlikely in the near future."

Uncle Matthew chuckled. "She is not very subtle, but her heart is in the right place."

As they entered the drawing room, he took a look out the window. "I had intended to travel home today, but I fear that may not be possible if the weather is about to turn. I have no desire to be stranded in a snowstorm on the road."

"You can always stay with me at the cottage."

"No need to inconvenience you, my dear. The colonel has already offered to put me up for another night if the weather turns nasty. So very kind of him, don't you think?"

"Yes, of course."

Uncle Matthew smiled. "A fine fellow – old school, you know. Not like these young harum-scarum fellows you meet everywhere these days. I'm glad he bought the old place. Your father would have approved. We had a good chat when I arrived last night and again this morning over breakfast. His plans for the place are ambitious. But you probably know all this already."

"Unfortunately the colonel does not confide in me, and I have little influence." Uncle Matthew raised a brow. "Not that I should have, obviously. It's none of my business."

"He would be a fool not to take your opinion into account. No one loves this place as fiercely as you and Mary. Well, my dear, I must go to the stables and consult my groom." He squeezed her arm as he departed. "I'll be back shortly."

Kate walked over to the window, watching the clouds thicken on the horizon.

"Do you mind if I join you?" a lady asked, coming to stand beside her. It was Mrs Woodgate. They had been introduced earlier by David, but had not spoken more than a few formalities. Up close, Kate was struck by the close resemblance between mother and son. She had the same dark, almost black eyes, straight nose and natural haughtiness. She looked every inch the matriarch, but her voice held warmth. Much to her surprise, Kate took an instant liking to her.

"Please do, Mrs Woodgate. Have you enjoyed the day?"

"I have very much and it was all so unexpected. Robert did not inform me until the day I arrived that he was hosting a wedding. I thought I was coming to spend a quiet Christmas with my son."

"I'm sorry your plans have been upset."

"Not at all! I love company above all things and who does not enjoy a wedding? I must congratulate your sister on her wonderful choice. I don't know David very well, but when I met him last summer I thought him most gentlemanly."

"Yes, he is and I believe they will be happy together. I will miss Mary, but she isn't moving far. Hanbury is only five miles away."

"Is it as pretty a place as Malton? I must confess to being pleasantly surprised. My son's letters told me little, but this is a fine estate and I hope to explore the surrounding area during my stay. Perhaps you might care to be my guide?"

"Certainly. It is a pity you are not seeing it in summer. The walled garden here is quite exquisite," Kate said. "It once held the finest collection of old roses in this part of the country."

"Your family lived here at one time, is that not so?"

"Yes, and my mother planted up the rose garden. But I was eleven when we left. My most vivid memories are of the nursery floor and the garden."

"I'm sorry. It must be difficult to come back to this house as a visitor."

"No indeed, I'm not sentimental about it. It is a little sad, but that is more to do with the manner of our departure all those years ago."

Mrs Woodgate frowned. "Why so, if it is not too impertinent a question?"

"It was a traumatic event, you see. Each year my parents went to town for the season, so we were used to not seeing them for months at a time, but we loved it here and felt safe, I suppose, in our familiar surroundings. But unfortunately one year while in town, they both contracted influenza and died within a week. They are buried in Kensal Green."

"My dear Miss Hamilton, how dreadful!"

Kate swallowed hard; her parents' deaths were something she rarely spoke of. "Thank you. The servants informed the family and within days my aunt and uncle arrived and we were bundled into a carriage and taken to Bath to their home. I recall the servants coming out on to the steps as we departed and I could not understand why the women were crying. It was only when we reached Bath they told us the reason for our abrupt departure. We lived there with them, very happily, you understand, until Mary turned eighteen and we returned to Malton."

"What happened to the estate while you were minors? Was it held in trust?"

"No, I'm afraid my father left many debts and Malton Manor was sold within months. The new owners did not care for the place and rarely stayed. They neglected it dreadfully. It was a huge relief to everyone in the village, including ourselves, when they decided to sell. We had returned to become tenants in the village, to a cottage once owned by my father."

"That cannot have been easy."

Kate shook her head. "We love Bramble Cottage. It is old and ramshackle, but we have had six happy years in it. It is perfectly situated, being next to the school where I taught for some years. I will miss it when I leave."

Mrs Woodgate's brow shot up. "If you love it so much, why are you leaving?"

"I must support myself, ma'am. I hope to find a new position after Christmas. I had to leave my last employer under a cloud."

Mrs Woodgate indicated a sofa close by. "Won't you sit with me? I would like to hear about it." She listened while Kate told her about Mrs Cartwright and her time in Bristol.

She tut-tutted. "The country is full of women like that. Thank goodness Robert stepped in."

Kate bristled. "I was about to resign anyway. He just happened to arrive before I had a chance to do it."

Her arm was patted. "No doubt he thought he was doing the right thing. He has a strong sense of honour."

"It didn't stop him being vastly disagreeable about it for the entire journey home."

"He doesn't like to be thwarted, like most men, and

Robert is a proud man," Mrs Woodgate said. She gave Kate a searching look, which reminded her greatly of the son. "I wonder if I might impose on you?"

"Certainly, but I'm not sure how I can be of assistance," she said as her hand was taken.

"My dear Miss Hamilton, would you permit me to call you Kate?" Kate nodded, wondering where this was leading and feeling uneasy. Mrs Woodgate sighed heavily. "I am very worried about Robert. I have only been here a couple of days and I am shocked to see how withdrawn he has become. I assume you know he was badly injured in Africa. He came back to us in a terrible state with a bayonet gash to his neck and a bullet wound in his leg. But as soon as his fiancé saw him, what does the goose do, but declare she could not bear to look at him and swooned on the spot. She broke off their engagement the following day. Naturally, he was devastated, although I will confess I always thought there wasn't much between her ears. I nursed him through the worst of it, but although his wounds healed, it was his state of mind that caused us most concern. Then one day, out of the blue, he announces he has bought this place and within a week he had packed up and left us. We were worried, of course, but my husband felt it was the best thing for him to make a fresh start. Then about six months ago, his letters stopped for a while and I became concerned. About this time, Robert's father became ill so I could not leave Kent. But I wonder, can you tell me if anything significant happened around that time? I have asked him, but he dissembles with nonsense about being busy."

Kate felt her stomach twist. "I'm sorry, I have no idea."

"I rather hoped he had found someone to replace Alice. Would you know if there is anyone in particular …?"

"No! I have been away from Malton, Mrs Woodgate, so I am the wrong person to ask."

Thankfully, the guests were scattered about the room, chatting away and no one could overhear their conversation. She looked up to see if her uncle was in sight, escape to the forefront of her mind. Instead, she caught Robert Woodgate staring at her and his mother from across the other side of the room.

Mrs Woodgate leaned closer. "Are you sure, my dear? I may be old, but there is nothing wrong with my eyesight. Robert has played the host well today, talking to all the guests, making sure everyone is being looked after. But he is avoiding your company. Now, why is that?"

"I have no idea," she said, panic rising in her throat. Was the universe conspiring against her now?

"Yet, his eyes never leave you," Mrs Woodhouse said.

She did her best to recover. "Most likely it is because he is waiting for me to do something indiscreet, for he enjoys telling me off. We frequently disagree, you see."

Mrs Woodgate sat back, a smile lighting up her face. "Ah! Now I understand. You present a challenge." Her grip on her hand became tighter. "Then my instincts are correct."

"Ma'am?"

Mrs Woodgate took a deep breath, followed by a shaky smile. "Please rescue my son."

Stunned, Kate sat staring at her. "Whatever do you mean, ma'am?"

Mrs Woodgate continued as if she hadn't heard her. "Now, it would be fatal to show any pity, for that will remind him of Alice. How crushing pity is to a man's ego, don't you think? You must force his hand, my dear. Find a way to break through those defences he has built up."

Her dark eyes bored into her and Kate became flustered. "I'm sorry, Mrs Woodgate, but I ... must find my uncle."

Head bent, she slipped out of the room, but she felt awful. The look of disappointment on the lady's face had touched her heart. But what right had she to lay such a burden on her?

Walking rapidly, she made her way towards the small drawing room to the side of the house. So caught up in her thoughts, it was only when she stood before the French doors she realised her destination. With a trembling hand, she opened the doors and stepped out on to the terrace. The years fell away. The rose garden.

The air was impossibly still and she knew snow was imminent, but the draw of her memory, the draw of the roses was too much. In her mind it was midsummer and the hybrid teas were in full bloom. Her mother was smiling indulgently as she and Mary chased each other around the rose beds. The air was heavy with scent, the buzz of the bees hypnotic. For a tantalising moment it was real, but then she felt the first flake of snow land on her cheek. She brushed it away with a shaking hand and opened her eyes. But her mother was gone. A stab of grief punctured her heart.

But at least the old stone walls and the beds were still there. It looked as if someone was taking good care of her mother's legacy. The rich dark soil was heaped with manure for the season to come. The branches of the bushes were stark and sad now, some with frostbitten hips still clinging on, but she could imagine how they would flourish in the spring once they had been pruned. She stepped down on to the gravel path and slowly made her way down between the beds, stooping to read the names. Her mother's planting labels were long gone, but the names of the roses were familiar: *Reine des Violettes*; *Boule de Neige*; and *Souvenir de la Malmaison*. How extraordinary they had survived. How wonderful!

As Kate rounded the corner of the house she came upon a scene of panic. Many of the guests, afraid they would be trapped by the weather, were hurriedly departing. The snow was getting heavier and the wind was starting to rise. It was only four o'clock, but the light was failing fast. Kate would have to hurry home, too, but first she would have to take her leave of her host and her uncle.

She found Uncle Matthew deep in conversation with Mrs Woodgate in the drawing room. They fell silent as she approached.

"Ah, my dear, there you are. I was afraid you had left

without saying goodbye," he said. "Come and join us."

"Please do, Kate," Mrs Woodgate said with a kindly look. "And it is all arranged. You cannot possibly go back to that cold empty cottage tonight. You must stay here. I'm sure your uncle would welcome your company."

Kate sat down, feeling as though a trap were closing in on her, but short of begging the colonel to take her home, she was stuck. A sudden snow-laden gust shook the windows. Fate was definitely working against her. It was now blowing a blizzard outside.

For the best part of an hour she sat and listened to their conversation, periodically joining in. But she was exhausted and longed to escape. The house grew quieter around them. Tea was served. A maid came in and lit all the lamps and banked up the fire. Kate wished she had gone home to the familiar surroundings of Bramble Cottage. She felt on edge.

"I do wonder where Robert is?" Mrs Woodgate said, turning to Kate. "Would you be a dear and see if you can find him? I'm sure he has sneaked away to his study."

"Then I doubt he would wish to be disturbed," Kate said as lightly as she could manage. Mrs Woodgate's gaze took on an intensity that was almost frightening. So that was where he had learned that look, Kate thought, with a sense of impending doom.

She exhaled slowly. "Of course, I'd be happy to."

Once out in the hall, she closed over the door and leaned back against it. Her heart was pounding as if she stood at the top of a precipice. But she had never baulked before, no matter what the obstacle. Hadn't Hamiltons fought and survived Waterloo, for goodness' sake? Praying for inspiration, she slowly walked down the hallway. She knew well where the study was, the memory of their last confrontation popping uninvited into her mind.

Taking a deep breath, she knocked on the door then slipped inside. The room was dark but for the light of the fire and a solitary lamp on the desk. He was sitting forward, staring into the flames in his shirt sleeves. His jacket was flung carelessly across the back of the chair and his injured leg was stretched out and resting against the fender. He didn't look like a man who wanted to be disturbed. She cleared her throat and waited just inside the door.

Half-turning, he looked up at her. A flicker of surprise crossed his features, then his face closed down. "Miss Hamilton, what can I do for you?"

Formal, cold and blunt – how typical, she thought. Why did he have to be so disagreeable? "I wanted to take the opportunity to thank you, on behalf of Mary and myself. It meant a great deal to her to be married here." He grunted, looking slightly uncomfortable, then he waved at the seat opposite. "No, I won't disturb you, but your mother wishes you would join her in the drawing room."

"Does she indeed and why does she send you? Have my servants lost the use of their legs?"

"I'm merely the messenger, Colonel. There's no need to take your ill humour out on me."

He sat back in the chair. "You are mistaken, Miss Hamilton, as you so often are. I'm not cross. Standing all day is not comfortable for me. I'm resting my leg."

"And you must do that in private, hiding away in here? You fought for your country. I do not understand why you are not proud of your injuries. Surely, they are a badge of honour?"

"No one wishes to see deformity." He turned away.

"That is self-pitying nonsense, and you know it."

"I beg your pardon!"

"Isn't that the reason you bought Malton Manor in the first place? Somewhere safe to hide away from the world. Isn't it time you stopped feeling sorry for yourself? I, for one, am getting tired of it!"

He straightened up and glared at her. "If your object is to goad me, you are a fair way to gaining your objective. Though why you would be so foolish is beyond me."

"I've dealt with recalcitrant ten-year-olds and a witch in human form. You do not scare me, Colonel," she said, crossing her fingers behind her back. Provoking a reaction was a dangerous tactic. Would she be found buried in the rose garden?

To her amazement, he laughed, but it had a hollow ring. "Miss Hamilton, you are the strangest creature! I suggest you return to the drawing room and politely inform my mother that if she wishes to speak to me she knows where to find me."

"You cannot be serious!"

"I assure you I am perfectly serious. My mother is playing games. I do not."

So he knew well what his mother was about. "You can do your own dirty work," she said and sat down opposite him. "I'm tired of being a pawn."

"How sensible of you! What shall we talk of, Miss Hamilton? What are your plans? What will your next big adventure be, I wonder."

She knew he was being facetious and it hurt because she realised for the first time how much she wanted his regard. "I plan to leave for London in January. It is my best chance of securing employment in my present circumstances."

"Even without references? Or have you found a way around that particular problem?"

So much for him being in love with me, she thought. He's not exactly begging me to stay. "It's called taking a risk. Perhaps you should try it? After all, change and progress go hand in hand."

"Except when it comes to village schools and a board of governors."

Something snapped within her. Trembling with anger, she jumped up. "You are impossible!"

He leaned back in the chair and shrugged, his face blank.

Turning on her heel, she made for the door. But she was brought up short. The light was dim, but she recognised it straight away. It was her parents' portrait. Hanging in *his* study. She took a step closer. It used to hang on the return of the stairs. She reached out to touch it, then froze, her breathing rapid and shallow.

The likeness was exceptional even down to the laughter in her mother's eyes. As a child she had loved to look at it, particularly during those months when her parents were away in London. It had been a link to them and one she thought she had lost forever, only to find it *here*.

"Why do you have my parents' portrait?" she asked, spinning around, her voice shaking. "You have no right to it!"

"Kate!" He got to his feet.

"How dare you! It should not be here." Deep down she knew she was being irrational, but she suddenly needed to lash out, mostly because she was scared of the future. Everyone else was moving on and she did not want to be left behind in this limbo.

He took a couple of steps towards her, looking startled. "I will remove it, if it upsets you that much."

Appalled, she covered her face with her hands. "My God, I'm sorry. I don't …" She took a deep breath, but couldn't stop the tears. She stumbled towards the door, her hand scrambling for the handle.

But he was beside her in an instant and his hand gently closed over hers. "Kate, please don't be upset." He drew her back towards the fire and somehow into his arms. "You've had an emotional day. Cry if you must," he said.

She tried to pull away, but he tightened his hold, resting his chin on her head.

He filled her senses. Through his shirt she could feel his heart pounding wildly. He wasn't as composed as he seemed.

"Did you not realise the contents of the house were never sold?"

"No," she answered, her words muffled against his waistcoat.

"Do you want to know why I had it hung in here?" he

asked, his voice cracking. He took a step back and looked into her face with such intensity she thought her knees were going to give way. "You are the image of your mother. I wanted to be reminded of you every day. When you left, it was all I had. My dearest wish was you would come back – I even made sure the gardeners took special care of the rose garden. I want it to be your rose garden, Kate." He caressed her cheek and his voice grew husky. "I don't want you to leave again. Promise me, please."

She nodded, finding she couldn't speak, nor look away from that hypnotic stare. In that moment the tension drained from her body to be replaced by something warm, safe and comforting.

Like coming home. At last.

He did love her. Slowly he drew his thumb across her lips, setting off fireworks throughout her body. He smiled, a roguish smile she had not seen before, which set her pulse racing. Then he kissed her. Gently at first, but with growing passion until she became light-headed. The hand cradling the back of her head was suddenly pulling out hair pins and she felt the weight of her hair as it fell down her back. His other hand was straying down her back and pulling her closer.

"Ahem."

Kate had not even heard the door opening. Robert stiffened and they pulled apart a little, looking towards the door.

Standing framed in the light of the hall was Uncle Matthew and behind him Robert's mother, peeping over his shoulder.

"Might I suggest you unhand my niece, sir. I believe you and I need to discuss this situation right away," Uncle Matthew said, sounding outraged, but his eyes were alight with mischief. Behind him, Mrs Woodgate's shoulders were shaking suspiciously. They had been outmanoeuvred by their scheming relatives, but Kate was too happy to care.

Something which sounded very much like a growl came

from Robert, but he turned to her with a raised brow. "I don't believe I am willing to let the lady go until she accepts me. I love you, Kate."

"The lady finds the proposed arrangement very much to her liking," she answered and was kissed soundly.

"Bravo!" squeaked Mrs Woodgate.

Robert rolled his eyes impatiently and turned towards the door. "I do not believe any further discussion is required. You may close the door as you leave," he said to the intruders.

"Are you sure about this, Kate?" Uncle Matthew asked, his hand on the handle of the door.

"I have never been surer of anything in my life," she replied with a smile.

The door closed over with a gentle click.

"I thought they'd never leave," Robert said, drawing her to him. "Now where were we?"

After several minutes, during which he demonstrated his true feelings, he said. "You find yourself in a most fortunate position, Miss Hamilton."

"Is that so?"

"Yes, I do believe the scullery maid just handed in her notice and I am prepared, just this once, to employ someone *without* a reference."

"That is most unfortunate, sir, for *I* find I am otherwise engaged."

The End

Acknowledgements

Special thanks to my wonderful editors, Hilary Johnson and Fiona Hogan, for their patience, advice and professionalism.

Thanks also to my fantastic beta readers, Lorna O'Callaghan, Terry O'Callaghan, Karina Coldrick and Joan Sheedy. Your support and feedback is invaluable.

If you enjoyed this anthology, please post a review. Thank you.

Also available on Amazon (Kindle and paperback):

The Bowes Inheritance

Autumn 1882: Louisa Campbell, living in genteel poverty in Dublin, is surprised to learn she is the new owner of the Bowes Estate. When she arrives in England, she discovers her nearest neighbour, Nicholas Maxwell, wishes to continue a vicious feud over her land and the uncle she inherited from was not what he seemed. When a Fenian bombing campaign comes close to home, Louisa finds herself a prime suspect and must do all she can to protect herself and her younger sister. But who is really orchestrating the Fenians' activities? Will Louisa have the courage to solve the mysteries that Bowes Farm holds? And most importantly of all, will she ever be able to trust and love the man who is surely her sworn enemy?

The Bowes Inheritance was shortlisted for the Carousel Aware Prize 2016 and awarded the B.R.A.G. Medallion in 2017.

Would you like to know more? Chapter One follows …

The Bowes Inheritance

Chapter One

Idrone Terrace, Blackrock, Dublin, September 1882

It was late afternoon. A biting north-easterly was blowing in off the Irish Sea as Louisa Campbell descended the steps from her aunt's house. But she was impervious to both the weather and the magnificent view of Dublin Bay. It had been an incredible day. She walked briskly past the row of elegant villas as she made her way back up to Main Street to catch the No. 6 tram. She tightened her woollen scarf and checked her hat pin was in place, more from habit than awareness of the squally conditions. Still bemused, she battled her way on to the crowded tram that would take her back into Dublin. She spied the last vacant seat on the bottom deck and slid into it with a sigh of relief. The open top of the tram was not the place to be on such a day. With a jolt, the tram moved off, and as she stared out the window at the windswept streets, all thoughts of her aunt melted away. Those braving the elements were hurrying homeward, heads bent, holding on to their hats as the wind whipped about their ears. Nature was determined to rob them of their dignity, she thought, before her mind returned to the remarkable discoveries of the day.

Her reflection twinkled back at her from the window with barely suppressed mirth. A day that had promised nothing but mundane chores and worry over her sister's failing health had turned into an extraordinary succession of startling revelations. She could so easily have missed the letter that morning. Eleanor had been ill during the night, and on a whim she had decided to go to the confectioners to find a treat to tempt her poor appetite. Their lodging consisted of three small rooms on the first floor of a Georgian terrace house in Herbert Street. Down in the hallway, she had paused to sort through the morning post, piled high on a rickety table inside the door. The dusty fanlight above the door provided very little light and it was difficult to distinguish the names on the envelopes. The letter had been redirected so many times that the name was almost illegible, but the direction was Peter Campbell, Esq. – her deceased father. She inspected the envelope carefully, holding it up to catch the light. The postmark was Carlisle and it was dated six months previously. A leap of apprehension made her stomach turn over as it was most likely an English creditor looking for payment. She briefly considered returning upstairs to show it to Eleanor, but in her sister's present state it would only add to her distress. She quickly stuffed the letter into her reticule and hurried out into the weak afternoon sunshine.

She loved the hues and earthy scents of autumn, and Stephen's Green was a favourite place for her to enjoy them. The park's pathways were a quiet and tranquil oasis in the centre of the bustling Dublin streets. But today she was oblivious to autumn's display and sought only the seclusion of a bench, where she could read the letter in private. Something about it screamed officialdom and it bothered her. Clearing her father's debts had taken every ounce of ingenuity she had, including selling almost anything of value they had possessed. Now every spare penny had to be saved for Eleanor's doctor's bills. There was no cure as the damage to her heart, after rheumatic fever, was permanent. That was an insurmountable fact. Eleanor could not help feeling ill and she could not blame her for succumbing to occasional gloom, but sometimes she wished to escape it all – the responsibility, the dread and her own guilt. With both parents dead, they survived solely on a small annuity from their grandmother's estate, which barely met their day-to-day needs. They were condemned to live in genteel poverty, belonging neither to the high society world of the protestant ascendancy that should have been their birth-right, nor the honest straightforward life of working women. It was a heavy burden. If she made one wrong decision it could bring their world crashing down.

When she finally sat down, she held the envelope in her hand and stared at it, overcome with anxiety. But how bad could it be? Taking a deep breath, she broke the seal, and pulled the stiff white sheet of paper free of the envelope. She saw with a sinking heart that it was from a solicitor's office. But as she read its contents with increasing astonishment, she realised that instead of misfortune what she held in her hand was a ray of hope. Real hope. The letter stated in stilted legalese that her father had inherited an estate in England from a Mr. Jack Campbell.

It was extraordinary. Was it a mistake? She had never heard of this man. But the letter had definitely been for her father. Mesmerised, she sat pondering the startling news with a pounding heart. She would have to find out who this unheard of benefactor was, and there was only one person who could help her. This called for a visit to Aunt Milly. It was not a thing one did lightly. Her aunt, despite her soft and fluffy name, had been christened by their late father as 'The Gorgon'.

As her aunt's long-suffering butler announced her in funereal tones, Louisa vividly recalled childhood visits to the house in the company of her mother and sister. Those dreaded duty calls had always been uncomfortable at best, sitting in rigid fear of doing or saying anything out of place. Any slips in decorum were pounced on by their hostess and left their mother despondent for days afterwards. Their father had always had a pressing engagement that coincided with his wife's monthly visit to her sister, and on their return home, he would tease them endlessly about taking tea with Medusa.

The drawing room faced north with a view of Dublin Bay, but it was dark and oppressive, despite its opulence. The room paid homage to showy ornament on a grand scale. A particularly vile stuffed owl surveyed the room from beneath a glass dome. Its yellow eyes seemed to follow you about and Louisa could never feel comfortable under its gaze.

Aunt Milly, sitting ramrod straight in a chair before the fire, looked up from her book with a slightly pained expression. In spite of the tepid reception, Louisa dutifully kissed her aunt's proffered cheek and sat down; she was well used to her aunt's disdain. She knew her resemblance to her father's family, her chestnut curling hair and blue-green eyes, chafed her aunt.

Still in her early fifties, Aunt Milly was a formidable woman, always dressed in unrelenting black with her raven hair, streaked with silver, pulled back tight from her high forehead. An incongruous white lace cap did not in any way soften the effect. She was tall and gaunt and her very posture suggested a woman in a perpetual state of disgust with the world. Her strong opinions tripped off her tongue with ease, leaving most mortals utterly crushed.

Aunt Milly was the only member of her mother's family Louisa had ever known. She suspected avid curiosity had been the reason for her aunt's interest in her family over the years. Aunt Milly had sensibly secured a very eligible man, who was twenty years her senior, and dissipated to a degree that guaranteed she would not be bothered by his company for too long. There had been no children. The unfortunate Campbells' swings of fortune had been entertainment for a woman who was both bored and selfish.

"What brings you here, young lady?" Aunt Milly asked. "It must be at least a month since I saw you or Eleanor. I suppose you are both far too busy to visit your poor aunt."

She bit back the retort she would like to have made, and

forced a smile. "We knew that you were planning a holiday, Aunt. How are you keeping? You look in excellent health."

"I am tolerably well, thank you," Aunt Milly said. "I spent a couple of weeks down in Bray. The sea air did me the world of good. It's such a refined place and all my friends take houses there for the summer months now."

"How lovely," she replied. Not for the first time, she marvelled at her aunt's pretensions. Her house was literally across the road from the sea and its beneficial air; what difference a few miles south could make was a mystery.

"I take it Eleanor is ill again," Aunt Milly remarked, after a few moments of awkward silence. To Louisa, it sounded more like a rebuke than genuine interest in the health of her sister.

"Yes, she was poorly during the night," she answered.

"So, no improvement?"

"Not really. She has some very good days – sometimes weeks at a time. But the weakness always returns."

"Perhaps you should try a sojourn at Bray. There is a very nice hotel on the esplanade."

"We cannot afford it," Louisa snapped, fully aware that mention of money would annoy her aunt, but unable to prevent her irritation showing at the woman's insensitivity.

Aunt Milly swiftly changed the subject. "So, I assume you have a particular reason for visiting me today?" Her tone was cold but her curiosity was obvious. Her bird-like eyes glittered with it.

Louisa removed the solicitor's letter from her bag and handed it over without a word. Aunt Milly stared at her for a moment before putting on her glasses and perusing it slowly.

"Well, well, well … Jack Campbell dead – hah! Who would have thought he would do anything worthwhile," Aunt Milly sneered. "I thought him gone to his maker long ago."

She was shocked by the vehemence of her aunt's reaction. "But who *was* he?" she asked. "I've never heard of him."

Her aunt folded the letter and stared off into the middle distance, a queer smile on her face. "I'm not surprised. He was the devil incarnate – that's who he was."

She sighed impatiently. "But what relation was he to my father? He never spoke of him. Is he a cousin?"

"No, not a cousin, Louisa. Jack was his eldest brother," Aunt Milly revealed with all the triumph of someone who loves the power of knowledge, "and a complete scoundrel with it. He was the reason that Father forbade your parents' marriage."

"Gracious! So he is my uncle! What did he do that was so terrible? Is that the reason Grandfather Dillon took so strongly against the Campbells? I always believed it was because they lost the estate."

Aunt Milly looked uneasy and took a moment before answering. "It gives me no great pleasure to tell you this," she began with a look that belied her words. "It must be over twenty years ago now. Your uncle had to leave Galway rather urgently, with various unsavoury rumours flying around." She sniffed with distaste. "There was talk of gambling … and an altercation of some description. He was just like his own father. The apple doesn't fall far from the tree and he proved it tenfold. They tried to hush it all up, but loose talk cannot be stemmed."

"But surely my father did nothing to merit such harsh treatment as well? He did nothing wrong."

"How can you be so green, Louisa? You know very well it takes very little to ruin the reputation of a family. Your uncle's actions only finished what your Grandfather Campbell had already begun. We all warned your mother, but she would not listen to reason, even after Father told her she'd be cut off. But Sophia was always a fool." Aunt Milly slapped her hand down on the arm of her chair, her face contorted in disgust at the memory. "An empty-headed, love-sick fool."

As always, she was deeply offended by her aunt's derogatory remarks about her parents, but could not afford to be distracted by her bitterness. She needed to glean as much information about Jack Campbell as possible.

"This man – my uncle - did he return to Ireland?"

"No, and no one wept I can assure you," Aunt Milly replied. She held out the letter for her to take, as if it were on fire. "We all assumed he had come to grief somewhere." She smoothed down her skirts, her face set, as if in memory of something undesirable.

"But he obviously prospered. To own a farm of over a thousand acres, he must have done very well for himself indeed."

Aunt Milly laughed, a dry grating sound. "He probably married money – duped some poor female and her family. He had the charm of the devil, that one."

"But that seems unlikely, if my father was his heir," she pointed out.

Aunt Milly considered this. "I suppose not. What will you do?"

"I shall have to write back to this solicitor and inform him that my father is deceased. I don't think there is anything else I can do."

"Yes, Louisa, you must do that, but don't you realise? With your father gone, you are probably your uncle's heir. You have no brothers. There are no male descendants." Aunt Milly sat back in her chair, a half-smile lingering upon her thin lips.

"I know that is a possibility, but these matters can be very complex."

"Then you had better write your letter quickly, in case there are other heirs waiting to pounce."

She smiled to herself. It was almost as if her aunt actually cared.

The tram journey seemed endless. Louisa was anxious to get home to Eleanor to share the startling news. The elderly lady beside her snuffled into a handkerchief and coughed noisily.

She inched away as inconspicuously as she could, trying not to show her distaste. She pulled the letter out of her reticule, unable to resist reading it again and thinking about her mysterious relative.

She wondered if he had resembled their father and, most importantly, what had he really done that necessitated his leaving the country. Aunt Milly's vagueness on the topic made her very curious on that point. It must have been something very shocking for him to be banished completely by his family and all of Galway society. This unknown uncle was becoming a very interesting character. Since their father's passing, their lives had been very monotonous, so she could not help but feel a surge of excitement. A genuine black sheep!

As her spirits rose, endless possibilities began to open up before her. Was this a chance to escape their hand-to-mouth existence? If she was the heir, it might be possible to sell the property and settle somewhere more beneficial to Eleanor's health. But she had no idea how much such a property would be worth or even if it would be possible to sell it as it might be entailed. She would have to trust that fate was being kind to them at last, and although it might all come to nothing, if there was any possibility that she was the heir, she had to pursue it with the solicitors.

The tram trundled past Blackrock Park, conspicuously empty of strollers, through Irishtown and into Ballsbridge. At the canal she hopped off the tram and made her way along the bank, still deep in thought. On reaching their lodgings, she felt a pang of guilt for leaving Eleanor alone so long, but hoped her good news, and the bag of macaroons she had bought earlier that afternoon, would make up for it. She gathered up her skirts and flew up the stairs, bursting into the room, unable to contain her excitement.

"Look, Eleanor, look! You will never believe it! And you will never guess where I have been this afternoon."

Eleanor shrugged, looking confused as she took the letter that was being waved in her face.

"Why didn't you light the candles?" Louisa scolded. She proceeded to do so, struggling to maintain her happy mood as tendrils of anxiety crept back into her consciousness. Even in the dimness of the room Eleanor didn't look much better than she had that morning. The shadows under her eyes stood out starkly purple and ominous against the unhealthy pallor of her skin. Her dark brown hair, limp and untidy, tumbled down over her shoulder, untamed by ribbon. She looked older than her seventeen summers.

"Good Lord!" Eleanor exclaimed when she had finished the letter. "Who on earth was Jack Campbell?"

"Indeed a very good question. I was never so shocked. He was Father's eldest brother."

"What?" Eleanor's eyes were wide in disbelief.

"Yes, I know. Isn't it incredible?"

"But I always thought it was just Father. Why did he not tell us about him?"

"It appears he wasn't terribly respectable. In fact, I suspect he did something dreadful. Well, it must have been for all the Campbells to be ostracised as a result," she said.

"Except by Mama," Eleanor said with a soft smile.

"Yes, luckily for us. Of course as soon as I read the letter I knew I would have to talk to Aunt Milly. Sure enough, she knew all about him, though I suspect she withheld the pertinent details. She looked very uncomfortable talking about him. I don't suppose we will ever find out what he did, and at this stage, it hardly matters."

"But aren't you curious?"

"Yes, of course, but who do we ask?"

Eleanor sighed. "I don't know. I have to admit, I always thought it odd that Mama and Papa hardly ever spoke about their families."

"Yes. I used to pester Mama about it, but when I realised how much it upset her, I stopped asking. I have always suspected that Grandfather Dillon was a tyrant. Wasn't it a very brutal way to treat your daughter? She couldn't help falling in love with Papa," she said.

Eleanor frowned. "So what does all of this mean for us? If Papa was this man's heir, do we have a claim?"

"It is a possibility. I could be next in line, but I'm afraid to hope. I shall make some tea and we shall have these," she said, holding up the confectioner's bag, "and I will tell you all I know about Uncle Jack."

Louisa left for the tiny kitchen, humming softly, but her good humour unsettled Eleanor. She frowned over the letter and was overcome with a sudden fear that something outside her control was about to change their lives forever.

29060989R00079

Printed in Great Britain
by Amazon